T0149230

My Love for That WOMAN

My Love for That WOMAN

Love happens when you least expect it.

Adrian Hamilton

My Love for That Woman
Love happens when you least expect it.

iUniverse books may be ordered through booksellers or by contacting:

iUniverse
1663 Liberty Drive
Bloomington, IN 47403
www.iuniverse.com
1-800-Authors (1-800-288-4677)

ISBN: 978-1-4917-7050-4 (sc)
ISBN: 978-1-4917-7051-1 (e)

Library of Congress Control Number: 2015909475

Print information available on the last page.

iUniverse rev. date: 06/18/2015

Acknowledgement

A special thanks to Caroline Harris who encouraged me, to continue writing when I wanted to quit, before reaching the end. I would also like to thank a very special friend in Trinidad, Rachelle Mohammed Lezama, for letting me know that the book was interested.

And most of all to my coach who told me that I had a story to tell after reading the first couple pages of the book.

Adrian Hamilton

Her breath was hot as the desert wind, as she blew into my ear, the warmth of her body felt hotter as she pressed against mine. The thrill of it ended very abruptly when the door opened and the presence of her little boy two years old stood in the door way crying Mommy! Mommy! I need you.

She left me sitting on the couch, walking toward her son she lift him up, hugged and gentle kissed him, while she took him back to his room, placing her son on his bed, and sang a lullaby that gently soothed him as he fell asleep. On returning she tried to continued, where we had left off, but the passion and fire that was burning within us fizzled. We sat and talked for a while attempting to rekindle what we lost back to life but it was no use.

It was getting late and knew I would have to leave soon, to catch my flight later that night for home California where my wife and children were waiting; it was just past eleven pm when I arrived at the airport and had half an hour to check in before my flight left for home. After checking in I called Didi as promised, but she did not answer the phone, maybe she was mad with me for leaving, but I had also promised my wife, I would be home and on that flight.

I got picked up at the airport on my arrival, just around nine thirty p.m not by my wife but a friend of the family, seems to me where ever I go people have been mistaking me for someone they know, because of the time difference from city to city I had plenty of time to go out, and still make it home before mid-night but the jet lag was taking its tole on me, since travelling for most of the week from city to city visiting the companies I was in charge of. Eventually, I declined the ride at the airport catching a cab, I headed for home, and felt as though I have been riding in the same cab all night, but it soon came to a stop right in front my door

As I entered the house greeting me my Sarah, and my two children Dawn My Daughter age ten and Matthew age five, this was a surprise to me because it had never happened before Honey! she said, how was your trip, this got me thinking, what does she know that I don't, it went quite well was my reply, except for a few minor details, we had some things to put in place at the Chicago office, how was your week. Fine dear! They were a major shake up at the office and released a lawyer.

Now children tell me about your week at school, the youngest said well, dad I did not do much more than the usual, in other words I said, you got into trouble again, yes sir! He replied, then the eldest, dad yes I said, the class had a field trip to the zoo, it was so boring, they were little to do, most of it were looking at the animals and listening to where they came from. After listening to the kids week in review, I tucked them into bed kissed each on their forehead, walked out the room and closed the door behind me, then it was just my wife and I.

I could sense that something was bothering her, but what it was I could not tell, I did not want to probe but to let her tell me what was bothering her, so I waited but nothing was said, does she know what happened tonight, I thought to myself is it possible. The more

I thought about it, the more it got to me I was now getting tired after my trip, and I could not put my finger on what was bothering my wife, so I fell asleep after twenty minutes thinking about the lady in Chicago. Next morning as I awoke, the kids came into the bedroom asking what we were going to do today, I have no idea! I said, what do you two like to do? We do not know either they said, now why don't you two go to your rooms and think about it.

After the children left the room my wife said to me, that I toss and turned most of the night, as if I was restless did I! Was my reply, yes Sarah said, my answer was maybe I was very tired, did I snore at all, no! Was the answer and I left it at that. All through the day I thought of what we had as a family, but something's seems to be missing, whatever it was I could not put my finger on it, so I left it alone, although it was still around in my mind.

The weeks went by so fast, that I hardly paid attention to the time. I had to go away again but this time, it was a week of seminars and I had to make a list of the names for the branch office that would have to be there. I know that my family comes first, but I could not help thinking of the lady I spent time with in Chicago. I made several attempts to contact her, but refrained from doing so. It was a matter of time now, when we would come face to face, with each other again, since she was going to be attending the week long seminar, and hopefully that there will be no disturbance this time.

At home, I gave my wife all the attention she needed, but whatever I did seems not enough, the family went to places they choose and we all shared jokes or stories with each other, and just having a great time. Sometimes I find myself day dreaming, and my wife will call and would pay no attention, the first thing that she would say is, who is it this time? That is occupying your thoughts, and my reply is that, there is a problem I was trying to seek out in my mind, to see if it is the way to go before presenting it to the office staff.

I had not given any thought to what my wife was doing at home with the kids, but somewhere in between having a shower and drying myself off I had the strange feeling that she may be doing exactly what I was doing. I tried to block it out of my mind, but could not, so I made a phone call to the children, to make sure all was well at home, when the phone rang Sarah answered it, and that was a relief to me knowing that she was at home. Sarah was tall in stature stood at least five feet ten inches, medium built, shoulder length hair, and brown eyes in color, she have a light brown complexion and brown eyes.

We spoke for quite a while, and told her how much I loved he, after saying good bye I thought about what I was doing to my marriage, but in spite of it all I was really in love with Didi (lady in Chicago) and could not shake the feeling of being deeply in love again. My training of thought shifted back again to Didi, and when she entered the bedroom after showering, and just the way she looked, made me felt in love with her more. I know how she felt and her feelings grew more as the hours came by.

The more time spent with Didi, the less I thought of Sarah, is not the same how I felt about her a couple months ago; sharing things are much easier with Didi than with Sarah. It may be that Didi and I work for the same firm, and knew more about the work that we do than Sarah although she and I have discuss lot of things and ideas together, I feel that I have to actually drag the answers out of her, and that this feeling I have is a sense of do not ask me anymore questions.

The time for me to go home to my wife and children were now winding down, and in about four hours, I will be on a plane home bound, not knowing what I am going to see or hear, as the time approached for boarding, the plane came around, I said good bye to Didi, and felt I was losing my best friend but knew I was going home to another best friend. Didi was tall and slender, with a great figure, stood around five feet nine inches, a figure most women would die for; her eyes were dark brown and had a bronze complexion,

Looking at Didi I had the feeling she was going through the same thing, except she was not going home to anyone but her son, which she spoke to me in length about and also her parent's and no arms to go around her. Our plane took off ten minutes after each other, and the sadness I felt went straight to my heart. I was also glad to go home after such a long week of seminars and the extra two days spent in Niagara Falls.

As the plane taxied down the runway my thought were on my wife, and the two kids, I did not buy them anything this time I was so deep in thought as to what kind of situation I was going home too, my mind began to play out situation some which I did not like, it was some of the same things I have been doing, although I knew it was wrong, because of how I was feeling at the time and the position I was in at present.

This situation was not only morally and ethical wrong, because of the commitment I have given to my wife when I said I do, looking back on the years when we were first married oh it was happy ones, but as the years came and went life began to change both our lives. We both have very different careers now, and most of the time we were out working and coming home very tired, time spent with each other was limited.

I think about all the fun times spent together, when we did not have any children, but now that the children is around we try to spend more time as a family, but it does not always work out, my guess it's the amount of work we both have to do. Am I feeling guilty, for not spending time with my family yes! But when duty calls one have to go and do what they have been ordered to undertake to bring order into perspective.

One of the things I miss most is the frequent going out to different events, around the state and country side, some of the most memorable occasion was at the county fair riding the merry go round. I kept wondering what I am suppose to expect on my return, is my marriage still intact, although I did not leave with the impression that something was wrong, but before leaving, sensed that something's was going on with Sarah.

In the distance I saw the lights of the city, and knew that in twenty minutes the plane will be landing, and taxing up to the gate, and soon I will be exiting, and be on my way home. I did not ask Sarah to meet me at the airport, at this time but took a taxi home. Sitting in the back of the taxi, on the way home all I could think about was Didi, then came some flash back of our relationship, and closeness that we have now, my thinking was so cluttered with feelings, emotions and other thoughts that I did not know when the taxi pulled into the drive way of my home.

The front light of the house was not on, and my only thought was that no one was at home, as I put the key into the lock to open it, the door swung open Sarah and the children greeted me in a way that I was never greeted before, on any occasion, this was very overwhelming and was so happy, because I did not know what I was going to meet when I got home.

Walking into the living room, my children was glad to see me, I dropped my suitcase kneeled to the floor and give them a big hug, then it was Sarah's turn but noticed she turned her face away I immediately jumped to the conclusion, something was going on in her life, she does not want me to know, how ironic. I questioned m myself does she have an inclination that I am seeing someone, on the outside, or is she seeing someone or is she doing the same as me. Life was not normal until a few days later; I was at home things were a bit shaky, arguments came up about the kids, and work. It seems that every time I ask a question my head got chewed off, for no reason, and I stopped asking her any questions.

For the next couple days I made a promise to my kids I would come home earlier, and spend time with them, especially now that their baseball season was starting and their games will be on different days and would make the effort to attend all of their games as as possible, time flies, when you are having fun, for most part of the summer travelling was not frequent as before, most of the office staff would be spending time with their families, going on vacation. We had no plans to go on vacation this particular year, there were so many things to take care of around the house.

During the school vacation we had great fun and other days were not so good, they were times I wish time spend time with Sarah, was with Didi and my son but it just could not be, Didi understood and maybe one day in the future our summer vacation would be spend with her as a family the time came and went so fast, summer was almost over, our weekends were planned, visiting family went going on picnics and outings with a packed lunch, and fishing with the kids, Sarah did not enjoyed fishing the children accompanied me, because they enjoyed the outdoors and love eating whatever fish was caught.

Most of our planned weekends were not enjoyable, Sarah had to cancel, the fact is she had to go into the office to work on something, so we went without her where we had planned, or who we had to visit, on many occasions we over night when we visited family returning the next day. This went on for a while, whenever she planned something I cancelled, so she can experience what the kids and I felt when we went out, not as a family unit. In spite of all the planning it seemed so obvious, that she did not want to participate in any planned events, but wanted us to participate in those events she planned.

I could remember one summer, my brother, and his family came to visit, and my kids had a baseball game on the same day they arrived, that evening. My sister – in – law and her kids decided they would go with me and watch the baseball games, when we were leaving Sarah came home, and asked me to wait for her, and I said no! The only reason she wanted to go was my sister-in-law was here visiting, and felt left out being by herself home alone.

I made a point of letting her know that the reason she wanted to go and watch the kids play is because my sister-in-law was here, and on no other occasion that the kids played she showed an interest, all she did was dropped them off and visit her friends, and returned later to pick them up when the game was almost over and that was selfish of her.

Summer was coming to an end and although Sarah did not participate in much of the planned events, the kids and I enjoyed ourselves tremendously, and as the summer came to a close we had already made plans for the fall season. It was now early September, school was about to begin in the next couple days, they were shopping for school books, and clothes for the kids to look good and well groomed, on their return to school from the summer holidays, and the beginning of the school semester, which means new friends, to be made in a new class.

Although we in the south did not experience the fall season as those in the north, I knew what the fall season was all about, with cool days, and the changing of leaves colour into that of a bright golden hue making the landscape of the surrounding area and rolling hills an awesome sight to behold, which can leave you breathless at times. The weeks went by so quickly, that it was almost the end of September, and was anticipating going out of town again planning company's strategies, for the following year, on the last Friday of the month we received a letter, from my in-laws that they were planning a trip to visit us.

This was the first time they were paying us a visit, and was the second time they were going to see their grand children, this was okay by me, but I was not going to stop my trip or halt any of my plans just because they were coming. The weeks came, and the day for their arrival was getting closer, preparation had to be made, and the spare room had to be cleaned, and put away so they can occupy it, when they came. It was now the day of their arrival, and off we went to meet them at the airport, all four of us, driving to the airport was silent, you could hear a pin drop, no one said a word to each other not even the kids spoke

Because of the quietness, I had to say something to break the silence, by asking what are you all thinking. They were still some silence, but finally someone spoke or muttered something to the effect as why today of all days? I paid no mind, nor gave it any thought to why it was said. The plane did not arrived as schedule they were a little delay, because of some bad weather before they left, this gave us a little time to talk about what was bothering the whole family, in the beginning all was happy Sarah's mother my in law and the kids Grandparent were coming for a visit.

Now, as the time is here I am second guessing that it was not a good time for them to pay us a visit, but this could not be reversed, no one answered the question that was asked, not even Sarah, my sentiments were that she may have had other things on her mind, and now may not be the right time for them to come. The plane finally touched down, and it was announced over the loud speaker, they were still no excitement, but that soon changed when in our sight through the glass appeared her parents, waving as happy as a lark.

After collecting the luggage's, they entered the waiting room, where we were, I greeted them, not with enthusiasm but with somewhat less of a general greeting, but made sure that I kissed my mother-in –law, the kids did managed to greet them in the manner most grand children greet grandparents, the table were now turn to my wife, and the greeting she gave them was not what I had expected.

I got the bags and headed to the parking lot, where the car was parked, the kids followed me and bringing up the rear was Sarah, and her parents, what they were talking about I hadn't a clue, but Sarah happened to break a smile but that was all. The kids sat in the back of the van, and Sarah's parents in the middle seat, driving home they were a bit of giggling, breaking the silence. The wind was a bit chilly and as it blew into the van the scent of perfume, took over; the fragrance reminded me of the type Didi wore.

We arrived at home half an hour after picking up my in-laws, and as we entered the house, Sarah's parents were so amazed. The way the house was put together, since buying the house we did extra work on it, and put a deck to the back of the house, that overlooked a homemade pond, and a flower garden. After relaxing for a bit we all had supper, and sat in the living room, and had tea. The children sat around talking to their grandparents before being excused to get themselves washed, and ready for bed.

We sat and talked for a while after the children went to bed. We talked about the weather, their trip and anything that was happening in the neighbourhood, and how was life on the whole, but it seems to me life on the whole emphasised more on us, with not much more to add, we called it a night and turned into bed. Morning came fast and felt as though I did not get a good night's sleep. The week end was on us and nothing was planned, but the kids wanted to have the usual weekend breakfast, at the family restaurant, so we all walked to it which was only ten minutes from the house, giving us the opportunity to get some exercise.

We all sat down for breakfast, and planned what we were going to-do for the weekend, and agreed, to visit the aquarium, and take a walk in the park, was the only plan for today, which was Saturday, but we still had to plan for tomorrow Sunday. The day turned out to be perfect, the sun was out in its splendour and lots of people was out doing some jogging as we headed for the aquarium and the park, the kids always get anxious, because they enjoy the outdoors and especially the aquarium.

We had a very good day outing, and after walking the park we were off for supper at a Mc Donald's, because, Sarah and myself were too tired to even think of going home and cook, Sarah's mind seems far away as though her thoughts were on something else, she was a bit quieter than normal than any time I have known her. Her mother did not know what to think, because Sarah hardly said much to her, as though her mother was in her way, whatever she wanted to do.

I did not ask Sarah what was wrong, but knew if something was wrong, she would say so things were left the way it was.

The weeks came and went that it was almost time for Sarah's parents to return to their home, Sarah's parents did talked to her, but what it was about I had no clue, but things looked a lot different now that her parents were leaving, it took a while, but she did happen to smile more often. The day came for her parents to leave, and Sarah, decided that she did not want to go to the airport, and say farewell to her parents, but stayed home instead the children came though, and had a good time on the way to the airport.

Dawn was a child after her dad, her hair was black, and had brown eyes, love to laugh and have fun, her skin tone was slightly brown but would not change it for the world. She had brown eyes and a smile to die for, very friendly to anyone

Once we returned home the kids went into the backyard and play, leaving Sarah and me to talk, she refused to talk about what was on her mind, so I left it at that. I tried changing the subject and talked about her parent's visit which had little response, and any kind of communication I said! It is okay if you do not feel like talking about it, and walked out the room leaving her all to herself. I watched the children, saw how happy the children were, and joined them in the backyard, playing tag and one on one basketball, for the weeks that followed we played in the yard occasionally, sitting and talking about school, and the new friends they made since it was a new school year.

The weeks and months came so fast, Sarah had not told me what was bothering her, and I did not preyed, if she wants to talk she will can approached me and we can have a conversation but was not to approach her. It has been four months since returning from the seminar in Buffalo, and in the next couple months, will be visiting most of to the branch offices I am in charge of, but could not wait to visit the Chicago office to see Didi. We had kept in touch every week, talking to each other about twice a week, letting her know how much I miss her and cannot wait to be with her.

Since Sarah was not talking to me about her problems, I made a suggestion that she see a counsellor, it did no good, she did not think anything was wrong and said she was fine! I began depending more on Didi, as someone I can talk to, since becoming closer with her, found myself not wanting to give any kind of indication to Sarah about was going on with me, and what was taking place at work, because it did not matter, she paid no attention to what I had to say.

In the following years, they were visits from both sides of the family, not much was said about the problems we were having. I could speak to my parents about anything that was bothering me, but had no clue if Sarah could talk to her parents the way I spoke to mine, they were concerns about our marriage, not communicating was one of the hardest thing I had to go through in my relationship. At this point during the year, I made a decision to move out of the house, so Sarah can have space and time to think, things over with me not being there bothering her, but had second thought leaving the children.

Matt was skinny but very fit for his age did lots of sports, and his best was soccer then baseball, stood about four feet five inches has black curly hair and light brown skin tone

Talking to Sarah became so hopeless that I would come home from work, change my clothes, grab something to eat and go into the room that was converted into an office and stay there doing work late into the night just so that I would not have to make any contact with her. Things got worse as the days went on, and at this time began staying out late and coming home just before bed time, our sex and married life began to deteriorate to the point that the children knew something was wrong, between their mother and me, but did what all parents would do, we shield them from the truth, assuring them that everything was okay, and mom had something's she had to work on at the office causing her stress.

It was just a matter of time; sooner or later the truth will emerged, but could not wait for that day to come. My calls to Didi, was much frequently and was giving her reports on how things were going at home with Sarah and me. Every time we talked I could hear the eagerness in her voice wanting to see me again, and once again the planning stages for meeting all personnel from the branch offices that I am in charge of was drawing closer, and I was in a happier mood to get on the road again.

The dates for the meetings were set, and called Didi, letting her know the day, flight number and time my flight was leaving, and if she could meet me after her word day was over. I left for the airport in a taxi for my flight at 3:30 pm after the kids came home from school, kissed them and told them how much I loved them, and that I would call and let them know when I would be coming home.

I arrived at the airport half an hour before checking in time, and had to wait for a while, I made a call to Sarah's office, to let her know that I was at the airport and all is well at home with the children, and that I loved her in spite of our communication problems, but she was not in, so I left a voice mail with all the particulars. After checking in my bags went over to the boutique and purchased something for my son, which I had with Didi, no sooner the purchased was made the flight was announced for boarding, it was 4:30 pm the flight took off as scheduled, as the plane reached its cruising altitude, I could not help thinking about Didi, and that longing feeling that was being carried seeing her again.

I began reading some memos that were in my briefcase that I brought along, and before I knew it, we were over Chicago sky line, approaching the airport to land, but the captain came on and announced that they were having problems at the airport, and that we would have to circle for a while.

Finally we were given permission to land, and as we taxied down the runway, my heart started racing as though I was seeing Didi, for the first time, after retrieving my bags exited into the waiting room, and there she stood, in a black dress sexy as ever, waiting for me, as she approached her arms out stretch, as our bodies were about to meet, I dropped my bags and briefcase on the ground, and gave her the biggest hug, and kiss that was ever given to anyone.

They were eyes on us from all corners of the waiting room, as we got into a passionate embrace, after that episode I picked up my bags and briefcase we headed over to the hotel, where I always stayed, in the same room, which was arranged differently, my usual drinks were all laid out, and as we sat on the couch we held hands, and locked lips again, and both our hands were all over each other, as though we were animals in heat.

We held each other, our hands moving up and down and all over one another, and could not wait to make love to each other, but in the heat of the moment we both decided to wait until we had time to talk to each other., taking a breather from each other we held hands and got into a conversation mode, asking questions about each other family and about our son.

After having such a meaningful conversation, we had a craving for some food and deciding what we wanted to eat I called room service to have our supper sent up to the room. It was a while before our supper arrived, and it gave us the chance to get our feelings out to each other (you guessed it). After supper we talked for another hour or so then decided to go over to her apartment, entering the living room sat her son, with his grandmother on the couch. I was introduced to her mother who was slightly grey and slim built, was very good looking, and my comment were, now! I know where Didi got her good looks from.

I handed the present which I bought for her son at the airport boutique, and as he unwrapped it his eyes seems to get brighter, and as soon as he saw what it was his eyes opened even wider, came over and thanked me. It was so good to see him again, and also to have met her mother for the first time. We all sat and talked for quite a while, asking me questions about my family, but she had no inclination that the person she was talking too was her grandson's father, my guess was Didi never told her parents who his father was.

It was time for her mother to get back to her husband, but before leaving extended an invitation to join them for supper before leaving Chicago, and to meet her husband I accepted, getting up and saying good night she headed for the door, and was off. We sat around for a while longer, and as it was time for me to get back to my hotel, all three of us headed for the door, got into the car and we were off.

As we drove towards my hotel, we passed a couple ice cream parlours, and I! Said, that the next time we came to one we should stop and have our self a treat, which we did. After the treat we continued to the hotel, reaching the hotel we both decided that it was late and that she would not come up but take her son home, and tuck him into bed.

It was Friday night, went up to my room, put the T V on to check out what movies or shows were on, made a drink, sat on the couch and watched a program, that I have not seen in a long time, just as I was about to relax the phone rang, and on the other end of the line was my wife, what perfectly timing, to be here, Hi! I said, are you all right? I asked, yes! She replied. I just call to let you know that I got your voice mail, and that I love you, thinking back I cannot remember hearing those words from her for a long time, Wow! I said in my mind.

We talked for about twenty minutes, or so it seems as though it was all a dream, but it was in fact real. I did not know what made her say that those words, but she did after hanging up the phone, my thoughts began to play out some scenarios is it real what I am hearing? Or is it all words and that she feels that I am owed those words.

In between thinking the phone rang again, but this time was a voice that was as soft and pleasant, if not gentle, that could calm any stress you may have, and at that end of the receiver was Didi, the woman my thoughts are on most of the time especially when I am not talking or thinking about my wife.

The gentle voice came as a surprise to me, because knowing Didi, the way we got to know each other it was no doubt, that she was going to call me as soon as her son was tucked in bed. Because it was Friday, and the week end, and we had no work to go to the next day, we stayed up talking to each other for a while, making plans for the next two days about what we were going to do.

Didi has never mention to her son that I was his father, but we had a close relationship, and every time we talked on the phone, or face to face, always ask me if I knew his dad, whenever I call his mother, and that he was interested in meeting him one day. Didi did not think that it was time to tell him I was his father, but she was hoping one day the opportunity would arise, and felt the same way, no one hoped that it would happened, but the way things are going at home between Sarah and me that opportunity may arise.

After our long conversation, we said good night and bye to each other, and saying our love you to each other click went the receiver and I was off to the shower before turning into bed. It was 2:00 am Saturday morning before I fell asleep. I awoke at 10:30 am, which was late, the way the bed was placed, and the drapes hung over the windows no light entered the room, due to the heavy blinds which gave you more privacy, and the look of a much darker room especially at night.

After shaving and having a shower, managed to get dressed and headed down to the restaurant for brunch, but before reaching the door the phone rang, and that gentle and pleasant voice greeted me, and you can sense the warm smile on the other end of the receiver, Didi call to say that she and her son was coming to join me for brunch since breakfast was over. It took Didi approximately thirty minutes from the time she called, to the time she arrived. I was glad for the company, since we had planned our day which includes her son, and now that we were all present we could leave in one car instead of me driving over to her apartment to pick them up.

Walking into the restaurant made me feel as though we were a family although I had a family already, being aware of the feeling we shared with each other, one of the toughest thing I had to consider was telling someone you came to know you are his father, Didi's son sat like a perfect gentleman, was well mannered, did everything he was taught, which he made me proud to be his father knowing the way Didi raised him to be who he is today.

The weekend was well spent, but it was coming to an end, and Sunday afternoon was giving way to the evening, although I spent time with Didi it was not the quality time that we usually spent, but having our son with us made it more enjoyable. Alex was a bit on the heavy side with dark hair, stood about three feet four inches, his eyes was light brown and a light brown skin tone with a great smile

It was time to return home after a long day of fun, sampling food at the food festival. Didi decided I come over to her place for a while before going back to the hotel, she made the decision to leave her car at the hotel, and pick her up in the morning, when we entered the apartment her son ran straight to the couch, lay down and fell asleep, giving us time to relax, with each other. It was a nice time unwinding with a glass of white wine and in the presence of good company.

Her son was now sleeping for an hour and a half, and it was time to put him in his bed to sleep, lifting him up I took him into his room and Didi changed him into his pyjamas, and kissed him goodnight, after tucking his blanket I looked at him, and his smile reminded me of the way my other son looked when he fell asleep. They were a similar trait in both of them, after walking out the door and closing it we sat on the couch and reminisce more of the day we had, our hands started to find each others, and the next thing we knew our lips was locked unto each other, something we both enjoyed when we are in each other company.

The constant touching made things a bit steamy, and our hormones began to get the better of us the next thing that was left to do was get into bed, and under the sheets, which we did, making love to Didi was very enjoyable, and having her in my life was even better.

My love life to Sarah, these past months was not as passionate, because we were not communicating to each other, and made it impossible to talk about sex, when we did have sex which was not very often, you had to make several advances to Sarah, if not they would be no emotion as to her wanting to have sex. Sometimes it makes me wonder if they was a problem with me, but knowing how things got when I was around, and no intimacy was shared often enough between us makes me wonder if they was someone else in her life too, and was bothering her more than me.

What seemed like an everyday occurrence for most married couples was in fact a difficult feat for me, which made me think whatever, was going on it is only a phase and things would work its way out. I stayed with Didi until midnight, and giving her a goodnight kiss left for my hotel, while on my way started thinking about where my loyalty was and on family issues. Is it my immediate family or can I be a family with Didi and her son?

Before going to bed I called home, and spoke to the children since the time zone was a two hours difference, just to hear how they were doing, and about their school work, after talking to them I asked to speak to Sarah, but she was not home, Dawn said! She was out for the evening, so I said! Tell her that I called and will call her back tomorrow. I had a hard time falling asleep, thinking again about my position with family loyalty, finally I fell asleep after a few minutes. I woke up a bit tired, but somewhat with a much peaceful mind, that does not mean putting it to rest, it will always be in the back of my mind.

It was about 7:30 am Monday morning; the phone rang, between having a shave and bath, hello I said! on the other end of the receiver, was Didi, telling me not to forget to pick her up for work. Soon after getting off the phone it rang again, and this time it was Sarah calling back to find out how I was since she did not talked to me last night. I did not ask her where she went nor did she tell me where she had gone, I figured it was not my business asking her. We spoke for ten minutes, and told her that I miss her, how much I love her but did not hear those words back from her, which left me thinking again about family loyalty, and where her love priority lies.

After getting off the phone, I had enough time to have breakfast and pick up Didi for work so she can get there before 9:00am., on the way to work we talked about what she would like happen between us, but we did not get to finish the conversation. My day at the Chicago office was very busy, getting together with the manager and his supportive team in planning for the year and the future. We had mini meetings through the day, and doing problem solving within each department making sure that they all work as a team to accomplish our goal for the future.

Didi had a busy day also, she was involved in some or if not most of the problem solving team efforts, because she is good at what she does. We did see a lot of each other, but did not let anyone know we were involved. We had to work as professionals in our job capacity, and not as lovers or having people know that we were having an office affair, but after our work was done exit the building discretely.

Our week at the office was very chaotic, with little time to spare, and the weekend was approaching when I have to leave for California my home base, she made arrangements to spend a couple nights with me, and had her son stayed with his grandparents, because she was going to be working late, and left a phone number where she could be reached in case of any problems.

We had supper at a very quaint restaurant on our way to the hotel, and had drinks at the hotel bar, before going up to my suite, we had a night cap, around 11:30 pm before going to bed, when we did get to bed we could not wait to get into each other arms, and the ecstasy and passion that she showed me I immediately showed her how intimate I was by my affections for her.

The locking of lips and the adrenaline rush of making love to each other was so forceful, that our hands were all over each other, and at that moment the animal instinct came out, and the love making began with the sheets going one way and our bodies another. My penis got so hard that in the blink of an eye it was inside her vagina, and the moment of the in and out action taking place the climax reached its point. The ecstasy of the full impact of love making came to a boiling point, and with a loud sound we both sigh, after having climaxed together, lying on top of her, and my penis still inside of her relaxed for a moment before we cleaned up.

Making love was so enjoyable, it was 2:00 am in the morning before going to bed, falling asleep in each other arms, was good for both of us it had been quite a while before we made love, and I felt the need, because I was not having any sex at home with my wife. We slept way past our wake up time, which was 7:00am, and had to have a quick shower, shave and breakfast before leaving for work. It was such rushing around that we almost forgot our briefcases, which had our agendas for the day's meeting with the other staff.

It was a hectic day, at work it was Friday staff could not wait for the week end so they can start on anything they had planned, the meeting went well and all who attended had some input and was satisfied with the progress made for the week. The meeting was about over and all were ready to leave, and thank them for their cooperation. My weekend with Didi was also about to begin, as we walk out the door, although we did not made plans, we decided to spend it at the hotel, and do some shopping for a couple items before returning home to my children.

We had supper at the hotel restaurant a couple drinks, which took up some time, and left, for my room at 7:30 pm. It was getting darker as the evening progressed, but the room was already dark, because of the curtain that was in the room backed with heavy drapes, Didi made a call to her mother, to find out if she can keep her son for the night and that was ok with her.

I made a call to my kids letting them know when I would be at home, after hanging the phone on the receiver we both slipped into something comfortable, and the evening was spent in bed, getting intimate with each other as two adults would do, when that comfort level have been reached. The touching of body parts made it impossible to keep away from each other, and as things progressed, we became more comfortable, with each other, got into something that would make love making easier our birthday suits.

Once under the sheets and the excitements began we could hear each other breathing, as things got intense. I began sucking on both her breast, and she played with my penis getting me more excited, and into the mood, kissing her occasionally. I placed my penis into her vagina, and started the up and down, and in and out action while she laid and enjoyed every moment of our love making.

It was a steady action of having sexual intercourse with Didi as she began to climax she began to breathe heavier, and her fingers dug into my back as she had her orgasm, and just as she was finished I got to the point of ejaculating sperm into her vagina, staying inside her for a while until things calm down. I rolled her on top of me before we got cleaned up, and that was such fun for her, she began to get excited all over again, but she stopped the action leaving it for another time.

After cleaning up we both relaxed, and had a drink or two, while watching a couple movies, before retiring for the night falling asleep in each other arms. It was such a very tiring night that we fell asleep as soon as our heads hit the pillow. Next morning we awoke close to 11:00 am, and before getting out of bed had more sex, getting even more intense, and exploring positions we had never tried, it was such an experience we could not believe they were so many positions we never tried before until now.

It was tiring but after having orgasms we dragged ourselves into the bathroom and showered together, getting all dressed found our way down to the restaurant for lunch, before going out shopping, she called her mother, before going over to pick up her son. I did not go with her, but we met at the mall at 1:30 pm and shopped for items that I had to get to take home.

We shopped for four hours, then went out for supper, a movie then home before returning to the hotel, during the drive to her house I did some reminiscing about my married life, the way it was and all the things Sarah, and I did together before we had our children. The happy times we enjoyed then, it is now at the point of going downhill, although it appears our marriage is on shaky grounds to you, it is not so, there are some obstacle in the way which have to be worked out.

Arriving at Didi's apartment reality returned into focus, and realized that they are people both male and female are having the same problems as me, you might say big deal, to you it may be, but sooner or later you will realize what it is like, when a marriage starts to fade away, and out of your control. I brought the car to an abrupt stop, for what reason I do not know, got out and went up to her apartment, knock on the door, and it was opened by her son, she came towards the door greeted me with a big smile and a small kiss, letting her son see that his mother had a good friend.

As the door closed, I was questioned by her son, Alex for short (Alexander) and gave him answers he wanted to hear, a question that we were both withholding from him, at age five children ask so many questions, and always want to know as much as they can comprehend. The question he asked was so forthcoming; he asked if I knew his father, I said yes! How do you know my dad? My reply, I met him a long time ago, how come I have never met him? At that point I really wanted to tell him I was his father.

I looked at Didi and saw a little tear from her eyes knowing how much she wanted to tell him, but thought he was too young to understand what happened before he was born. I happened to change the topic on him by getting him interested in playing a game; he was a quick learner played the game go fish, Didi walked into the kitchen to prepare a snack.

When the snack arrived, the game was stopped, for a few minutes, then continued, as Didi watched us play they was a gleam in her eyes, for some reason I got the instinct of a mother's feeling, wishing we were a family all living under one roof, being able to tell him I was his dad.

The worse that was happening right now to Didi's son is he was growing up without a father figure around him, not knowing who he was, and where he lives. The only male person's he sees most of the time was his grandfather and me whenever I come to Chicago, it was getting late and he had to get ready for bed, saying good night to me he was taken inside to his room, where he changed into pyjamas, brush his teeth, and was tucked into bed, bending over Didi kissed him on his forehead, and said goodnight and closed the door as she left his room.

It was almost 10:00pm when we finished cleaning up the kitchen, and straighten out the mess we made playing cards, we talked for a long time then left, kissing her goodnight, asked if she and Alex would like to join me for breakfast at the hotel, and her answer was a definitely yes.

I arrived at the hotel at 11:45 pm after leaving Didi's apartment, approaching the front desk the clerk asked, if I was Drew, "I said Yes' and handed me a card with a message" all that it said was to call home. I made the call in my suite, and when the phone rang Sarah answered, her voice was calmer and she seems relaxed and sexier, which I have not heard in a very long time. the voice what I heard in the previous months, was not the same, but a change voice, she wanted to know when I was due to arrive, and would like to meet me at the airport with the children.

It was a shock to me, hearing what Sarah just said, that my jaw stayed open almost hitting the floor, okay I said and gave her the flight number and arrival time, just then in the background the children came inside making noise knowing my daughter Dawn, she asked to speak to me, following her my son Matt (Matthew), after hanging up the receiver sitting in amazement as to what could have brought on the sudden change in her. Was it something mentioned over the course of the past weeks?

It tool sometime for me to comprehend what had transpire to me from Sarah, and could not believe what I had just heard, and what has happened in the time I was away. I got to thinking all this time after her parent left she was or maybe have been seeing a counsellor trying to solve what problems she was going through at the time.

It felt good in a sense, and maybe even better for her knowing she had done something worthwhile, dealing with the problems she was having, and facing it head on, not sweeping it under the rug as if nothing was happening and all was well.

To me what seemed as a big problem to her it was small. By letting the little things fester, it grew into a larger problem; something she could not handled all by herself, but needed the aid of a professional. If she was hiding this from me all this time, it was well thought out, and planned, and was not suppose to know she was seeing a counsellor, now back to reality, how does it feel hearing her say I love you, astonished, because for a long time I was the one who said it to her.

I had to lie down for a while to find out if it was a dream, or reality, and pinched myself to find out if in fact it was reality. The word stayed with me for quite some time, even when I was getting ready to leave for the airport. It was difficult enough having to deal with no communication from my wife, and not having sex with her for some time when all was not going well, made the best of it, now since she said, that she was fine and now love me, it will be just a matter of time, but would have to wait and see, her attitude towards me when I returned home from this trip.

I got up bright and early the next morning, shaved, showered, and got my bags packed, went down stairs to the restaurant for breakfast all before 8:30 am. Returning to my room made a call to Didi, and her son, that I was on my way home, and I had a wonderful time with them, and will talk to her when I get to work. I also told her that I love her, and would see her again, saying good bye hung up the phone.

With my bags in hand, taking one last look around the room making sure nothing was forgotten, closed the door behind me went down to the main floor, checked out, and drove to the airport, after checking in got myself a newspaper, and began reading, soon after my name was announced over the intercom, I should returned to the information booth to pick up a message. At this point I was not expecting any and could not think who would leave one for me.

As I was leaving I received a message from Sarah, the children wanted to know the time of my arrival, making a call home, I spoke to Sarah gave her my time and flight number again, then said goodbye, as I hung up the phone my flight number was announced, that all passengers should now board. Within twenty minutes after boarding the plane was ready for takeoff, at 10:00am it taxied down the runway. I began thinking about what was taking place at home, because when I left home I had no knowledge of knowing what to expect on my return. I do know that I looking forward to see the changes in Sarah, if at all there were any.

For the time being, I was not going to play out any scenario in my mind, but let the chips fall where they may made myself comfortable for my flight home on the plane well relaxed, and rested. I contemplate on what I was going to do for the next couple weeks that were ahead of me. I dozed off for a couple hours, in between dozing and awaking heard a few announcements, my guess, it was nothing of importance, because I was not awakened by the stewardess.

After napping for two hours, awoke in time for a light lunch, and knew we did not have long to go, before we touchdown in California. The light lunch was an indication that within two and a half hours we would be approaching the California sky lines, and by the time lunch was over we would be seeing the horizon in the distance. I began reading the newspaper I had bought, looking at the horoscope, to my surprise, said that someone in the past will come back into your life, if you will give it a chance and let it happen. Talking about déjà –vu it must be a dream or something.

I had no other choice but to pinch myself, making sure I was not dreaming, but sure enough, it was reality big time, closing the newspaper, wondered what all this meant, and not for hell could make sense of it. I brushed it aside, and did not think of it again. The captain came on the intercom, announcing we would be in sight of the airport within ten minutes, and all was looking good for approaching the runway, soon after the captain got off the stewardess announced all seat belts should be fastened and trays in the upright position for landing.

The seat belt sign came on, the clicking of seat belts could be heard throughout the plane, and then silence took over, and then a thud, and knew that we had touchdown. The roaring of the engines together with the flaps being down the plane slowed before reaching the end of the runway. It was now 11:45 am California time. The captain announced that we have landed and it was nice having us onboard, taxied to the terminal bringing the plane to a complete stop. The doors opened and the stewardess announces that it was safe to leave the aircraft, taking all your belongings with you.

Once out of the plane I took a good stretch, and went to the baggage area to collect my bags, entering the exit door in the arrival area, was Sarah and the children, it was such a surprise to me, and even a bigger surprise seeing the way I was greeted by Sarah. It was incredible the way she looked.

I was greeted with a hug and kiss from Sarah, and hugs from the children, on the way home all wanted to know how things went in Chicago, and if I was okay, and glad to be back home, and all I could say was yes! Entering the house I was treated like royalty, Sarah wanted to do so much for me so I can see the changes in her, from what she used to be to what she is at this moment. It would take some time for me to get use to her changes, at this point I would have to go along with whatever she is up to, whether it's a game or not, was not for me to decide.

The next day, was Sunday I relaxed with the children outside, and swam in the pool, the sun along with the humidity made it somewhat unbearable to take Sarah was in the kitchen preparing some snack for us to munch on before supper, gazing occasionally from the corner of my eyes she was looking out the window very often. After snacking, Sarah decided to join us for a swim, it was a surprise to us because, and she had never done it before, a change maybe but for how long. I would not lose any sleep over it.

For most of the afternoon I relaxed, and played with the children, and later some of their friends from school, and the neighbourhood came over for a swim. It was fun seeing them get along, and having such a wonderful time laughing with each other. The children's get together finished around 7:45 pm as the last of their friends left Dawn and Matt began tidying up, the rain began falling not even a dark cloud in the sky, the heavy down pour lasting for twenty minutes, then suddenly stopped, and out came the sun for an hour, with the tidying up of the pool area completed, they went to their rooms and began getting their school gear, and clothes ready for tomorrow the beginning of another school week.

Everyone in the house was up earlier than normal. Something never seen before, we were all eager or something to start off early, and also allow me to get a head start at work before anyone else, if that was possible, all I wanted was to get there so that I can talk to Didi without any interruptions, before all the staff showed. The phone rang at Didi's extension, but they were no answer her voice mail kicked in, and hearing her voice again gave me a jump start for the day. I left a message and told her that I would try again later around 1:00pm their time 10:00 am my time, and hung up. The phone rang just as I hung up the receiver and at the other end was Sarah, calling to let me know that she was going to be late getting home, she forgot to tell me that she had two clients that was coming to see after their work day.

Communicating was not one of her strong points especially with me, and was one of the problems we always had up to a couple months ago and still is, she may be right she has change, but for our marriage to work we must communicate, one of the main ingredient in any marriage. I am going to reserve judgment, and continue with my every day work habits but would not tell her I was seeing someone, but would not keeping her in the dark, but communicating with her on something's.

The office staff had just begun strolling in occupying their desks one at a time, looking eager to start their day, after everyone was in placed a small meeting of the divisional heads were called to fill me in on what took place while I was away. The meeting was a formality to bring me up to the present day happenings, thanking them all returned to my office and began my work catching up on some paper work that was not done before leaving for Chicago.

I finally settled down to do some work, when the phone rang at the other end of the receiver was a familiar voice, it was Didi, she happened to call me, they was a matter she wanted rectified, about the meeting we had, and wanted to know how things were going. We did not talk for any length of time, but told her what had happened before I left Chicago after speaking to her the night, and all that she could say was oh! And how would it affect us now that she is making an effort to communicate with you. I do not know if it is real or not, was my reply, but was going about it as i would normally do, anyway I would call you on Wednesday of this week, since I am going to be working late, we would talk, ok! She replied, and hung the phone up.

It was quite a busy day at the office, attending to all the mails that I had not answered before leaving, and today's incoming mails and memos from the other department managers, together with some mini meetings on the spur of the moment notices, without any agenda in mind, I must say they went well. I did not even made an attempt calling Sarah at her work, knowing things seems the same, and she was working late, this gave me time to catch up on more paper work. It would be a matter of a few minutes that Dawn, and Matt, would be getting home. I left them a voice message informing them that Mom and I would be a bit late. I had better communications with my daughter, and son than Sarah, and tried instilling it as part of their values, it had to be done on a regular basis if it was going to work, and they must be no pressure of any sort.

I came home after a long and stressful day, changed into my swim pant, and headed straight into the pool for a swim before supper. I stayed there for at least forty- five minutes, and felt ok after emerging from the pool, had supper, and watched the news, after the news was over Sarah walked in said hello!, and went up to the room to change into something more comfortable.

Sarah came down to the kitchen, dished out her supper sat at the table opposite me, and did not spoke a word while eating. I did not say anything either, not until she had finished, she said how her day was, what strikes me as odd was, said she has changed, but was a bit of the same old person, not even as much as a touch or a kiss or asking me how my day was, it was all about her day.

It was getting to the point that I did not want to hear anything more about how her day went, so I made an excuse, and went to my home office to work on the computer. If I did not see and hear it, I would not have believed, exactly what she told me when I was in Chicago did not even took place. It was only the first day of the week, and if this is what I was going to see for the rest of the week, there were simple no change in attitude, was she trying to really change or is it a farce, on her part saying that she has. I have not seen it, the only thing I saw for the day was, she calling me, and informing me she was going to be late getting home.

I have come to terms with the whole situation, with whatever was happening with Sarah, and I would have to go along with her up to a point, if in fact there is a chance of uncertainty, in other words if there is no change, in her attitude then I would have to live with the fact the changes she talked, about was no more than a farce.

The evening was getting a bit darker, and came up stairs from the den to sit outside on the back deck of the house relax, while looking up at the sky as the clouds went by. I have not done this since a teenager, looking for objects the clouds made, but most of the time found me daydreaming. With my eyes open, and staring upwards at the sky and the cloud formation, I could not see any faces or objects I could name, with my eyes closed, did some fantasying about Didi, and how life would be if my marriage ever dissolved, not that I am looking forward to it happening, but at least one can dream or fantasize about things.

It was just about bed time for the children, 9:00pm the time they sat for themselves since they were in grade 3 and has continued since, after saying good night to the children, I came inside and read a magazine until it was time for bed, all this time Sarah was sitting opposite me in the living room reading a novel, and did not spoke a word to me since she came from work, and had her supper, the possibility was she had nothing to say, and left things alone.

I turned into bed at 11:30pm after watching the news, said good night to Sarah, and she did the same, no I love you or anything else, as soon as my head made contact with the pillows in less than five minutes I was sound asleep, they were no touching of any kind between Sarah and myself, each sleeping on our individual side of the bed without hardly turning.

The sun arose very bright the next morning, and the children were already awoke, getting ready for school, each taking turns using the bathroom, then we all met for breakfast. The children had they usual cereal, and my usual toast, tea and orange juice with an egg omelette, Sarah on the other hand had waffles, and orange juice, when we were finished the dishes were placed in the dishwasher, and we left for school and works, saying to each other have a good day.

On my way to work I kept contemplating if there was really a change going on in Sarah's life, and was I having any uncertainty about the change, because this morning she was back to her old self once again. I arrived at work fifteen minutes before my work schedule, and picking up the papers read the local section of the news, to see what events were taking place in and around the community.

The alarm on my watch went off, letting me know five minutes was left before starting my work, the office was starting to buzz with workers, mini conferences were taking place in and around the cubicles, discussing what problems had to be worked on for today, and which was top priority, everyone was well into their work by 10:00am, and sometimes it was so quiet as though everyone had lost their ability to speak, that was soon short lived, when it was time for coffee break came.

It was quite some time coffee break was over and lunch time was approaching. I had not made any decision whether I was going to stay in or leave the building for lunch, the phone rang, just before twelve noon and the manager from the accounting department wanted to know what I was doing for lunch, since he was going down stairs for lunch at the restaurant, and wanted to talk to me at that point I decided to joined him.

Before lunch was served, he wanted to talk about something that was on his mind, the problem was, he thinks his wife was cheating on him, what a question to be asking someone who is doing the same on his wife. He mentioned it was one of his best friends he had known for a long time. He received a phone call today from another friend who said, he had seen both of them walking in the mall holding hands. My question to him was simple this, do you believe that she is cheating, his reply, I do not think so, then you have to go with your gut feeling, until you have proof in your hand believe that she is not. We both went to our separate office's he the fourth floor, and me the sixth floor. My phone did not ring after lunch, but managed to get my work done especially those that were on hold while I was away in Chicago.

Being the second day of the work week, seemed very long perhaps it was due to the fact that I left home earlier that morning, but it felt good, and knowing the fact I did accomplished a lot of the back log paper work. The end of the work day was slowly approaching, and with it dark clouds, which could only mean one thing, rain with the possibility of thunder and heavy showers, before leaving work wrote a note to myself to call Chicago tomorrow and speak with Didi, as promised packed up my papers, and headed out the door. Before reaching the elevator door, I was called back, they was a call for me, at the other end of the receiver was my daughter's voice, she wanted me to buy her a couple of items she needed for a school project, she was working on, and since I was passing near the mall if it was possible can I get them, yes! I said.

The mall was quite busy for a Tuesday evening, so I got what I needed for Dawn's project, came right out, and headed home, parked the car in the driveway instead of the garage, because I was going to give it a wash, got into the house, and sat for a while before changing clothes even before having supper. After supper got the hose, and all the necessary things that was required for washing the car, and at that point Sarah drove up opened her side of the garage door, and not as much as a wave to acknowledge she saw me and show me that yes! They were some changes in her life.

I did not give it a second thought, but continued what I had set my mind to do, washing my car, while the children were doing their home work, and reading materials for the next day's school work. I stayed outside for a long time not wanting to go inside, but knew at some point I would have too, putting away everything that was used, walked in and all Sarah said was hi! Sorry I did not say hello to you outside, and my replied was it did not matter anyway. Her communication patterns was beginning to show again, and was not in any mood to point it out to her, she is the one that said to me she has changed, Sarah never knew how to communicate, which was handed down from her parents not communicating to each other, as much as they should, so it had an effect on her, in other words since her mother and father did not communicate it was ok to do so in the marriage.

Conversation was not one of her strong points either, which made it difficult for her to talk about anything, it is completely different when she have to talking to clients, informing them what they need to get done, and they listens, it is easier for her to talk with her co-workers, because they are not family, she talks to her close friend about everything, but I am not close with her friend, that I can ask her anything about Sarah.

I went to bed early that night to get a goodnight sleep, wanting to rise early, to be at the office, and have breakfast on the way it was around 6:00am when the alarm woke me up, had a shaved, shower, got dressed, and got all my things together, left for the office, Sarah, and the children, was still asleep.

Stopped at the restaurant for breakfast, arriving at the office at 7:45 am, no one was there as yet, and would have lots of privacy while talking to Didi, I called her from my office, with the door closed, this soft and sensual voice said hello! And immediately my heart skipped a couple beats, after saying hello I asked jokingly who was this although I knew who it was the moment hearing her voice.

We talked a while, and told her what was currently happening at home, and that I missed her and love her, and her reply was the same, something we said to each other every time we came face to face or spoke on the phone, that closeness we had with one other was there in the beginning, when we first dated in university.

It was no shock to me when returning home, the greeting Sarah gave me, was not convincing at this point I knew it was a sham, when she called me in Chicago telling me she has changed. I knew it was no way her changes could be true and seeing the evidence she portrait along with her actions.

Didi's voice was a welcome change, which gave me a lift all day not only today but every time we spoke, it was comforting. I was taken back on several occasions about walking out of the marriage, but I did not have the facts. I know how I felt for a long time but had the distinct feeling Sarah feels the same way, none of us for any reason or another want to make that move, maybe it is on account of the children, and the difficulty it would cause, that is a rift between both families which would be sort of chaotic.

I think of this all the time, walking away from the marriage would not be any problems, it has been quite a long time Sarah and I had fun together, We had fun before and after marriage, after the children were born things began slowing down, if and when that time for my marriage to end, I hope it is recognizable, in the mean time my marriage is still intact, and there is still hope.

In the months that follows, we began talking more with very little change if any, hoping to see a big change all at once, it was not in the cards, realizing in the last couple of months that drastic changes does not happen overnight, but had hoped it would happen. Still hoping and praying for a miracle things would happen in an instant, but it did not, but began to face that it is reality, taking life as it comes, one day at time, no matter what life has given me.

I did not stop praying and going to church with the children Sunday's, because of my upbringing in the Catholic Church, and my religious beliefs, unlike Sarah she did come with us on a regular basis. The only time she came to church was at Easter Sunday, she always had an excuse, that she was of a different religious faith which I think had nothing to do with what faith or denomination you belongs, faith is faith no matter the religion.

They were so much arguments about going to church as a f: but never did get her to come, I finally gave up, on the idea, it hitting your head on a brick wall, that did not matter anymo that I could do was keep on praying and hoping she would c her mind one day when we attend church on Sundays. The ide finally dropped, and never mentioned again, many times it cı my mind, but as the saying goes you can lead a horse to wate you cannot force it to drink, in my case is was exactly what doing.

We were married for thirteen years now, with the seven year gone, and over the problems began to get worse, as the day months came and went. Vividly I remembered one day Sarah to work and did not return home after 1:00am, with no explar given, no questions asked of her, acted as doing nothing wrong incident was left alone, this happened two weeks in a row ar separate days.

A couple of weeks past, I made reservations to get away from h flew to Chicago not telling her anything about my plans or I was coming back, left strict information with my secretary if she called to find out where I was she did not know, thi payback time, for what had happened in the last month fo inconsideration for all the things she had done.

Leaving bright and early Monday morning, after telling the chi bye and I will be off on a trip for a couple days telling then no about where I was going, knowing their mother she may ask if they knew where and how long my trip was going to be. arriving in Chicago four hours after boarding my flight, coll my luggage, and called Didi, she had no idea I was in Chicago was a complete surprise to her, she told me to wait at the airport would come and get me.

I was greeted with such a great welcome lots of kisses, and so n affection it had me feeling over whelmed, to get all that affectioı

was giving me so I returned the same affection, people stared, at us in the funniest way. After all the greetings we drove to her apartment, and she left for work, made myself comfortable, sat and watched the news and any other interesting news events happening around the city. Alex was not at home but at his grandparents, while Didi was at work. She had a good arrangement with them, they always wanted him to stay with them while she was at work, the day seemed as though it was getting longer, since dropping me off they was nothing to do but, time on my hands gave me much to think and reminisce.

Looking back on things in the past, I wished it could have been different, what I know now, had I knew then about the lack of communication it would have made a big difference before our marriage, although we used to talk for long periods at a time while dating, it is water under the bridge, what must be done now is try communicating with her the best way possible, this to let her know little of what going on with me. Sarah communicated with me less each day sometimes not at all; they were always laughter, and lots of talking between us in the first couple years of our marriage, because they were always something to talk about, now it seems a bit much for her to do.

In between reminiscing the phone rang, and this gentle voice said hello! It was Alex, who I have not spoken too in about a month how are you? Fine he replied, how did you know to call here? Mom told me that you were there so I called. How are your grandparents? Good! Do you want to talk to her Yes! If is that ok with you. Bye! See you soon as he holler to his grandmother phone for you!

We spoke for a brief moment, then said bye, just then they were the rattling of keys at the door, and the door opened standing between the door way was Didi. I helped her with her briefcase so she can have a free hand to hug me, asked her about her day and told her about mine, it was not quite 5:15 pm when she walked into the apartment, and it was a pleasure talking to her compared to Sarah. After putting things down we both advanced towards each other

hugging and kissing as though we have not seen one another for years, and was seeing each other for the first time. After all the hugging, and kissing we sat down she put her feet on the ottoman to ease the days pressure, sitting opposite took one of her foot, placing it on my leg started messaging it, while talking about what we were going to have or do for supper

We came to a decision that it would be a special evening she called her parents, telling them to get dressed; we were taking them out for supper. On our way over we stopped and got something for Alex, Didi choose she think he would like, as we drove up the driveway he saw his mother car started jumping up and down the absolute joy of seeing her was so much, I remembered when my daughter's actions was exactly the same when she saw my car entering the drive way. The car came to a complete stop, and before the door opened, he was hollering hi! Mommy! How are you? Coming out of the car and approaching him, he ran towards me, kneeling down gave me a big hug; it was a happy occasion seeing him, that it brought a little tears to my eyes.

After all the greetings, everyone got into the car and drove to the restaurant where we had reservations, each of adults had something different to eat and drink with our dinner, Alex wanted a hamburger and fries, soda instead of tea, after dinner, dessert was served, with carrot cake, ice cream and apple pie and a beverage of your choice, much to Alex delight, he had ice cream and cake and his favourite ice cream vanilla which he enjoyed.

It was around 8:30 pm we left the restaurant, and could tell that he was getting tired, having a full day at his grandparents, and having a good time at supper his eyes was now beginning to close, a sign that he was getting sleepy, all got up from the table in unisons and I went to pay the bill, while the others walked towards the car driving home after dropping his grandparents Didi's hand held mine a gesture of her affection, and appreciation of what was done today, which said that I love you in a kind of indirect way.

I fantasized being with Didi, and thinking, what life would be like having her as my wife, I applied the brake too hard, and the car came to a sudden stop, and was jolted back to reality. We had arrived at the apartment Alex was sleeping in the back, opening the back door gentle lift and cradling him in my arms, and took him up stairs, to his room. Didi came a few minutes after and change his clothes, and tuck him in for the night.

I watched her do all these things for Alex, realizing what a good mother she has been, kissing him good night as she has always done we left his room gentle closing the door without making any noise. It was not long before we both turned into bed, because Didi, had to work the next day since it was a holiday for me, I was not on official business we changed into our pyjamas, got into bed, under the sheets, her head laying on my chest, with my arms embracing her warm body next to mine, not knowing when we both fell asleep.

Next morning bright and early, there was a knock on the bedroom door, and before Didi could answer it the door swung open, and standing between the door frame was Alex, now five years of age, running towards the bed jumped, and laid between us until it was time to get ready for his trip to his grandparents house. As they both left the bedroom flashbacks were happening again, about life living with both of them, but was short lived, when she called asking "what do you want for breakfast?" anything that you are having I shouted back then a bit of silence throughout the apartment, next word echoed to me was, breakfast is ready come and get it.

Jumping out of bed put my robe on and headed for the bathroom, brushed my teeth, wash my face then the dining room for breakfast. Sitting together reminded me when Sarah, Dawn, Matt, and I sat as a family at the table having breakfast, it made me reflect how far I came and. thinking about walking away from my marriage. Excusing herself from the table she left Alex and me together for a while, this gave me a chance to have a small chat, he did not ask me about his father while Didi getting ready for work.

By spending a little time I got to know more about him, after eating he left the table and went to the bathroom, brushed his teeth, wash his face, and dry every part that was wet before leaving for his grandparents which was along the way to Didi's work. At 8:00am sharp they both left the apartment, said goodbye with a hug and she a kiss, Alex was dressed in jeans and a blue plaid shirt, she on the other hand looked so astonishing dressed in a beautiful pant suit.

I relaxed for a while took the dishes off the table, and cleaned up the kitchen, did the dishes, then took a shower before reading the newspaper, then took a cab to the shopping mall to purchase a couple items before lunch. The morning flew by fast hardly noticing the time. I enjoyed shopping by myself for a change, and that feeling of singleness returned, making me realized that it was fun shopping instead of having the whole family together.

My thoughts went back in time, to that of age twenty, when the university gang, and myself, will go shopping no one telling us what to buy, what matches and what did not, in my drifting backwards, and forwards time flew by when the sound of a clocks chime brought me back to reality, where and what I was about, stopping for a bite to eat, called Didi, informing her I was in the mall shopping and maybe home a bit late.

Just after talking to her I ran into an old school friend that I had not seen in over three years, his name was Charles, got talking asking all that typical male questions, what are you doing? Where are you working? And how is the family. Getting by all these questions and replying to them got us reminiscing of the good old days. This was short lived, because we both had things to do before a certain time, we exchanged phone numbers and addresses and promised to keep in touch.

I thought he would never leave l the way he was carrying on; it was just after 5:30 pm before I completed my mission and returned to the apartment. Didi was already home, and taking the keys out of my pocket to open the door, it swung opened, and was greeted with a big kiss dead smack on the lips, it was over whelming that pinching myself was the only way to make sure it was not a dream although knowingly I was at the apartment.

We sat on the couch holding hands, and began talking about our day, something that never happen at home, without any thought we were wrapped up with each other days activities, that the time did not remained motionless. It was almost supper time when our conversation concluded about our day's activity, after having something to eat she called her mother requesting if she can get Alex ready we were taking him for ice cream.

Watching Alex licked his ice cream cone reminded me the way I licked mine, all the way around before going to the top. It was a joy, and delight seeing them both making me think again about t them as a family, finally eradicating the thoughts out of my head, and realizing that it may never happen, maybe sometime in the future one never know about these things ahead of time.

It had never entered my mind to think, as a married person, I would be questioning myself about my marriage, and where it is going, should it be with my present wife and two children or with Didi and Alex. They comes a time in one's life, when you find certain personal matters are not going well on the home front, you may have to try your best making sure everything works by going for counselling, most times both parties find it very uncomfortable talking about their problems to a complete stranger divulging ones deepest and private thoughts.

Getting back to what is at hand, the mere thought of me considering the end to my marriage was not something I was planning, although things were going good on my side having the woman I dated in university, I cannot say anything was happening in Sarah's life. The thought was always there, but carrying out the action was a bit out of context. It would have to be under certain circumstances, facing the reality when it occurs, can happen to the best of us without any indication from our spouse.

I have known friends and some acquaintances that divorced had crossed their minds, and had a formula how they were going to draught up their plans when and if the time comes, as the saying goes the best laid plans sometimes does not work, this particular person who drew up his plan got a shock, when his wife told him unexpectedly she wanted out of the marriage, before he had the chance to tell her he wanted out.

It was such a blow to his ego, because he was dumped, and suffered from depression for a long period. I do not think that would happen to me, but one cannot tell the mind of a person, what I am talking about is divorce, all that can change instantaneously, when I took my vows it was for richer or poorer etc, etc, till death do us part but who knows when the parting will come. On our way home to Didi's apartment I sat quietly, for a few minutes, the first thing Didi asked was! Is something wrong, that intuition women have got into gear, sensing something was wrong.

My answer was no, a quiet moment was needed, I do not know or can give any answer at the time about what was active on my mind, but some bad thoughts came over me about what happened to the guy whose spouse told him she wanted out before he did. The car dropped into a pot hole, and jarred me from the trance or whatever I was thinking at the time, the first thing that came to me at that moment, was my wife and two children at home, and what were they doing.

Arriving at the apartment, lifted Alex up and took him straight to his room, placed him on the bed and Didi changed him into his pyjamas as usual, watching him lying on the bed, brought back memories of the time my times changing Matt's pyjamas when he was about Alex age, falling asleep before reaching home when we were out on long trips. After changing his clothes, Didi came and sat next to me, felt her warm body next to mine, and my heart began beating rapidly, because of the excitement she brings to my life. Very often wondering how life would be with her if my marriage was dissolved, and we got married.

With her warm body against mine, and my heart beating, took her into my arms, began kissing her setting off a rush of adrenaline wanting to make love to her right there, but told myself the time was not right, not that I did not wanted to, but we never said to each other lets go to bed and make love. There is a difference, between letting the passion, and adrenaline run wild as your thoughts are on that person who is in the room with you and would definitely make love too, on a bed while under the sheets, at the same time thinking about your children at home, would only affect the state of your mind.

They were times when all I did was think of Sarah, but since our problems started, and knowing Alex is my son and Didi is his mother they are no second guessing to what Sarah was doing at home, for some time now our sexual relationship have been tensed, and appears as though she never have the time or even wants too, so from time to time when I am here with Didi in Chicago every moment spend together with her is quality time and not quantity time which is a big difference.

It was a bit after 11:00 pm, and the words we have not mentioned which is making love came out, from both of us at the same time, taking her by the hand led her into the bedroom, both taking our clothes off, and stood naked in front each other, and within an instant we were embracing each other.

Gently laying her on the bed the passion and all that goes with making love caught up with us the way two people who love each other should be, the ecstasy that went along with making love to her was something that would not be forgotten. After our love making we shower together, and allowing the water to fall on our bodies while enjoying each other's company, something that was not done with my own wife in a couple of months, sometimes thinking about it hurt and the pain will always be there.

What hurts more is no matter how much I tried to be intimate with Sarah, they was always that distance, the closeness once shared was no longer in our marriage, but with Didi, she longed for that closeness, and the closer I got to her my feeling and my thoughts were on Sarah. The pressure of going through with all the hurt and pain was taken away being with Didi.

Getting to the point where my feelings were hurt had to be worked on, and as of now that have not bother me in a while, learning to deal with it took some doing on my part which lasted for a period of months. It has taken me quite a while to deal with the inconsistency Sarah showed, and the way we dealt with each other as a family; this is not saying we have a good relationship as we continue to live together. There are times my only wish were of being with someone who really cared for you and that is the place where I should be living.

I know where I am wanted, but my children also wants me, both needing a father as they grow, and needing some guidance. Telling myself things are going to get better as we go along these trying times seems so unlikely, dealing with our own problems on our terms and time is unrelenting with both of us feeling the pressure. As time went on they were no movement on the home front, and things began getting worst now that I am back from Chicago, communication between husband and wife was at a stale mate. The time spent at the house started dwindling more with Sarah, but found myself spending as much time with the children as I could.

We would visit parks sometimes as a family and visit friends; the one thing that was not on my agenda was visiting bars drinking and drowning my sorrows. At times my drinking began showing the effects it had on the children, making a serious effort not to drink on the week end, my weekends became much better, while spending time with the children watching them do their homework and playing with them in the backyard.

What was a burden, has now become a pleasure doing activities with Dawn, and Matt, going camping, hiking, watching them play baseball, and simple showing up to their activities wherever it took place. Home was still there, with not much being said between Sarah and me, they were things I had neglected on the house for a while was resumed, I started taking picture again, and doing sketches something I promised myself to get back into, when ever time was permitted. My wish was Sarah could join the children and me on weekend's outings.

It looks to me things would not get better, even as time goes by, as the saying goes things will get better as you age, anyone can read between the lines, and know that things may not get any better between us. I have given some thought of leaving, but kept saying the children are the ones to suffer in the long run if I walk out of the marriage. The feeling of abandonment and resentment would be a backlash on me, when you have not ever been divorced, before and hear the horror stories, and the vicious battles taking place between spouses you have to wonder why people don't stay married.

For some it is a nightmare, and others a smooth transition, I can only say, that life is lived from day to day, trying to make things go as smooth as possible, but time and time again I always return to the same question, why am I in this situation? When I can be by myself with no one to argue with, the answer always comes back to the children. As often as the question invade my thoughts, the answer cannot be given, since it has not happen yet, but will cross that bridge if, and when it arise, at the same time contemplating about a divorce, since Sarah, and myself are at odds with each other.

What it boils down to is how are we going to feel? What would the children do and think? When we do decide to get divorced, and go our separate ways. On many occasions talking to friends about what may happen brings chills to my spine, no one had any solid answers, since none of them had ever gone through a divorce. The more I think about it the more my mind was on Didi and Alex, and what are they doing at this point? I began to think rational now, having stopped the drinking, at first it was hard, but looking back now it was for my own good, because of what may have happen if provoked.

One afternoon I stayed working late at the office, called to Didi, Alex answered the phone it surprised me he knew exactly who he was speaking to, asked me how things were, and when would I be coming to see him, my reply was soon, he called his mother! Phone for you! After a long conversation, explained the situation at home and within a couple days I would be in Chicago, she was so happy and told me how much she missed me.

After our conversation, I made arrangements to fly into Chicago on the Thursday, did some more paper work catching up on any unfinished business needing my attention, working late into the night, not thinking about time and where it was going, no calls to home giving any indication I would be late, coming home. The task of completing and catching up was finished, all paper work, with everything packed and sorted which had to be distributed amongst the departments heads were left on my secretary's desk, then it was home bound.

Arriving home about 2:00am, relaxed for a bit, and went to bed without any explanation to anyone, morning came fast, it looked as though, my head had just rest on the pillow and had to get up, but remained in bed for a couple of minutes while everyone got ready for work and school, when all was quiet, got up said hi to the children, who asked me what happened last night, and had to give them an answer, after said good morning to Sarah, but all she said was oh! Hi! If this is all she can say why say good morning to her, it's just to be respectful.

When everyone left the house, I started getting ready for work, arrived much later than expected my ticket was ready and had to pick it up, today being Friday and would not have time to do so on Saturday. Usually it is the children's day spending time with together, although nothing was planned, anticipated where they may want to go, but it was a wrong guess, both wanted to venture on a long hike so it was agreed.

Saturday morning came, sat and had breakfast; we made plans as to which park we would go for the hike, and for how long. No one said a word at this point they were more interested with what they were eating. Breakfast was part of the weekend ritual, where we all sat together, since during the week everyone did their own thing for breakfast, time was of utmost importance everyone was so much in a rush that all you heard in the morning was good morning, have a good day bye, and see you later.

With breakfast finished, some muttering began to take place, and the question was where they would like to go hiking. All agreeded we would go to our favourite spot near the Midway Pass, that looked over the water falls at Duke's point. The morning began a bit gray, but as the sun came out the day began to improve, with the sun shingling brightly, and hitting our skin the heat from our body began to excrete droplets of water as though it was raining.

They scenery was breath taking, with the luscious green vegetation on the trees, and the green grass on the ground where the animals grazed, we had a few minutes layover then headed onwards, and came upon a smaller water fall where we sat on rocks each one picked their own, had sandwiches and snacks we brought along with us. It was not long after eating our snacks, and sandwiches we headed for home on our way back down the path, we greeted other hikers as we passed, seeing lots of different people hiking, was an experience that will not be forgotten.

By the time we got home everyone complained how tired they were, and sat down for much needed rest then jumped into the pool to cool down, before thinking what we were having for supper. A vote was taken, and it was agreed we should have be hamburgers, and hot dogs, done on the barbeque, and it was my job to do the cooking, and the kids decided that they would do the cleaning up after.

The entire day turned out to be a great one due to the sunshine, we all had fun while hiking, enjoying each other's company for a change, although my wife is not much of an outdoors person, she had to admit, she had a good time hiking, being her first time hiking with the children and me. As the evening was coming to a close, and the dishes done we gathered in the den, watched a video we rented, with popcorn made, we sat watched the movie vey attentively without saying a word to each other.

The movie ended, made the final house security inspection, and said good night to each other. Lying in bed next to Sarah, although we slept on the same bed, it showed how far apart our relationship had drifted, and the way we talk to each other at times, my thoughts were on the situation we were both in at this moment.

I do not know if the children are aware how much their mother and I have drifted apart. We continued showing them we still talk to each other, but deep down inside it hurts, after all these years it may come down to us not being together. The love we once had is no longer there. I thought of Didi while drifting off to sleep, and counted the days when it would be time to fly to Chicago, although I was hard for me to not keep in touch with her and Alex was hard, made sure never to call her from home, in that way the situation is not provoked.

It had never crossed my mind that one day at this point in my life, wished things would work out in a bad way, and it would come down to me saying, my hope was our marriage never existed so I can move in with Didi. My opinion on marriage is old fashioned, and would continue to stay that way, until something happen to change the situation. The mere thought and notion of me getting a divorce at this point is not something that can be wished, but the way certain events taking place around the house it may be a possibility.

If for one moment, they were situations that was noticed or any signs shown, I do not have a clue what I would do, if it came to be, having seen what divorce have done to families. I do not wish it on anyone, although we may think that we have control over it, we can fight, or come to some understanding with a spouse to seek counselling. Over the last couple months nothing has changed at home, and the way things are with Sarah, she tends to do her own thing, instead of with the family, which tells me she is selfish, and does whatever she wishes.

Observing the children's behaviour is another thing that has changed, they tend to get on each other nerve more often now than before, this may be due to their age difference, and friends they associate with, Dawn the older of the two is twelve and Matt is seven years. All this brings back memories for me while growing up, with my brothers, and sisters we all had different friends, some were older than others, but at times some rivalry took place when the younger siblings tried to fit in with the older sibling's friends.

It has been a while since I had spoken to Didi, and Alex, but it does not mean I am not thinking of them, when I am with them the comfort and easiness feels good, or it can be put this way it's a sense of calmness, unlike the stressful situation felt at home. Thursday was here at last, and went straight to the airport for my flight to Chicago to visit Didi and Alex, the usual greeting and affection was always there when spending some quality time with them. I was not staying for a long; it was a couple days getaway that was needed.

I returned home that Sunday afternoon and was back to work the next day bright and early, it appeared to me while working the time went by very quickly, before one can say Wednesday it was here, as always the weekend was a couple days away and was looking forward to it, so I can catch up with some planned yard work which had to be completed this weekend, as the weekend approached, my thoughts were putting the yard work off although the work had to be done.

The children always looked forward to the weekends, but this weekend was different they both wanted to do nothing which was ok with me. At times you tend to wonder if the children had picked up on any vibes that were being emitted between their mother and me; they were not any reason to, since we kept it on a friendly basis, so they feel comfortable at home. It always bothered me when Sunday's came around Sarah did not wish to attend church with us as a family, the children and I continued going. The only time she would attend church was during Easter and Christmas.

The question never came up why she did not wanted to attend church on other Sundays, it is just the way she was, it was never like this, when the children was smaller, we attended church every Sunday, now that the children are older she declined from going. Sunday afternoon was spent quietly, up until supper time, when the neighbour children came for a visit with Dawn and Matt, swimming while the evening sunlight was still bright.

There was so much laughter in and around the house that it took away the edginess that was hanging around. They were a glimpse of a smile coming from Sarah's when she turned to me as my head was raised the same time she turned, and it was a good to see a smile on her face, since it was not something she has-been doing frequently. It is a shame how someone as gentle as her can be so cold at times, which left me thinking, that there is something brewing in her mind, at this point no sort of indication was shown by her at all.

Still all were having a good time laughing, and as the day came to end pleasantries was shared by all there, it was time to say good night to the neighbours and friends as they left one by one. It is sad in a way, seeing the pleasant smiles on Sarah's face, but it soon came to an end, and that cold look came back on a beautiful person, along with it the frown lines across her forehead, and the house came from an evening of laughter to one on a cold day at the North Pole.

The children did their usual night routine, after saying good night to their mother and me, went upstairs to their respected rooms telling each other good night, and love you words to each other. As the night came to an end, turned and try making conversation but they was not much effort made to carry on a conversation, this being said, stood up left the room, and went into the den, remaining there for a while doing some heavy thinking about what can be going on in Sarah's head.

We have been married for almost eighteen years, and you think by now you should know your spouse inside and out, all the little quirks you can guess about her, like what she is thinking about, but this time clues were not seen or can be pinpointed as a tell tale sign of what she was thinking. Monday morning came so fast that my eyes looked as though it was closing down, since doing a lot of thinking about almost everything especially the expression that was seen on her face.

It was not a happy look, one that was never seen before, was I assuming something or was it nothing, making me think that? Did I see something to warrant it, could have been nothing, but at this time you get irritable? But it was taken to mean something to me. It was a bit confusing for a while, but could not help thinking about it. The fact that seeing what was there remained etched on my mind.

I did not confront Sarah at all, but left things the way it was, not mentioning anything at all maybe it was a good thing at this point, I tried blocking it out of my mind, and thoughts while at work, and to thinking about the positive, and not the negative. It was a bit quiet at work today, and scheduled a meeting for the Wednesday with all the departmental heads, to find out where they stood with everyone, and if they were any problems in their departments.

At the end of the work day, decided to do a little more work. I stayed a bit late not thinking clearly, forgot that today was Matt's basketball practice, and it was a good thing I called home he had just arrived home and wanted know where I was, and if I had forgotten about his practice. After hanging up the phone drove home, and got there in nick of time to take him to his practice, luckily for me it was not too far from home.

As we drove to the gym Matt asked me how was work? And replying to his question asked him how was school? And right out of the blue asked me if anything was wrong with mom, why? Have you noticed anything out of the ordinary? Yes! Was his replied, she has been acting a bit strange lately, how do you mean? She was sobbing the other night, and, I did not what to make of it, thanks for telling me, I would try and find out what she was crying about, practice went well, and when it was over we stopped for an ice cream cone, and chat for awhile.

We haven't had a family meeting for quite a while due to the amount of work Sarah and I had, and it may have been a good excuse not to have one then, fearing that it may bring something up that I may not want to hear. At the family meeting we gathered around the table, and each one said what they had on their minds, all gave their opinion on the issues, but Sarah could not say what was bothering her, gave somewhat of explanation to some problem, which had no bearing on the family issues.

After the meeting was over, and the kids left the table I approached Sarah to find out what was really bothering her, and she could not say, but it was something she was dealing with, and had to try solving it on her own without my help or anyone intervening. With no other explanation it was left at that, and did not asked for any time line when she could come, and let me know what was bothering her. I told Matthew that to my knowledge I did not have any idea what was bothering his mother, and left the answer hanging in the air, and she would let me know when she is ready to talk about the problem.

As the weeks went on Sarah appearance began to be noticed, she was wearing more make-up than usual and Dawn was beginning to observe changes in her mother's dressing styles, which was a bit provocative in nature, she asked her mother, what was going on? and her mother replied nothing! Since nothing could be done to help Sarah solve her problem which was consuming her, the children, and I did not bring it up. We carried on as though life was normal, and the house was run as it usually ran.

It was a couple months later when I noticed Sarah's strange patterns ways that were never seen, but paid little attention to it, until much later, suddenly it hit me like a ton of bricks. All this time thinking it was nothing it may have been in front of me, but going over the things that was in front of me the last couple months, came to the conclusion something very serious was going on with her, and did not know how to express her thoughts on the matter.

My initial thoughts was not thinking about anything bad, but deep down managed to put two and two together, and came up with what maybe the problem, Sarah is having, an affair, and did not want to believe it at first, but had no choice, but confront her with my assumptions. If my assumptions turns out to be right then life as a whole would have a different meaning so is our marriage. It never came to mind what the outcome would be confronting her and how it would turn out, but at this point my intention was not to back off.

My mind flashed on Didi, everything was on my mind at the time what if it turns out Sarah is indeed not happy, and wants out then some difficult decisions would have to be made. My mood at the time was quite, calm and peaceful. I was not in any way ready to start an argument, after giving it some thought decided to hold off approaching her for the next two day, just to get my mind at ease for any arguments that may arise from our talks.

In the days that followed called Didi, telling her what my thoughts were, and what I was about to do, she reminded me it may be nothing to worry about, but if things got to the point of getting nasty her place is available, and I can stay with her for a few days.

Sarah came home with a pleasant smile and said to me, she feels like making love later, this came as a surprise to me, where is this coming from all this time we slept together she did not wanted to be touched then out of nowhere bam! She wants to make love tonight Wow!

The night came and yes we made love but could tell the passion and ecstasy was not there she was not into it as before we got married, we both cleaned up and showered separately then went to bed saying good night to each other and back to the same sleeping pattern no questions asked. Next morning it was as usual as thou nothing happened last night, I challenged myself to be strong, and look at whatever is going on facing whatever the situation, in a positive way instead of going into it saying negative things or even bringing up past issues.

The day came I promised myself to asked my wife what was really going on, and why no matter what was tried, was not successful, although I promised not to push her, deep down inside, I had that right to know, and so were the children.

It never dawned on me to think that Sarah could have found out about Didi, unless someone told her, knowing no one was told about Didi from me and whoever it was did not hear it from her, so if that was the case why did Sarah made love to me? was it to find out if my sex life had dwindled or did she wanted to make love to me because she felt a bit guilty? I may never know, to my knowledge Didi has never called the house.

I asked Sarah to come into the den, because it was time to have a serious talk, whenever she was free, looking back on the past months while sleeping in the same bed, barely touching each other except the night we made love which was recently. It was the only time our bodies came together after months of sleeping on separate sides of the bed.

When she was free she came into the den, I simple asked her about the problems, and how I can help, she looked me in the eyes, and began crying, for a bit she, dried her eyes, and said the problem was me. Me! I said! What have I done? Nothing that is exactly it I don't think I am in love with you anymore. I have been seeing someone from my law firm, my jaw dropped, all I could do was stand there astonished not saying a word, looking outside with my back to her.

I could not believe what Sarah said to me, although the chance of that happening, and coming true was now a reality. I could not say anything; the thought of what I have been doing all along is reality that was manifested to me also. Now that it came from her, and straight out of her mouth, it pierced me in my heart, which was deadly with intense pain. I was not a saint myself, because of the things I was doing behind my wife's back. The unexpected reality of hearing that you are not loved by your spouse is not only a blow to your marriage, but it's the final episode of a marriage that lasted for twenty years.

I asked Sarah, how long was the affair was going on? She replied about a year, the person she was having the affair with, was someone I knew, and was at our home on several occasions. At this time it was a terrible blow me, and had no words to say, still in shock, and very much in denial of what was transpired to me by my wife. I did not want to believe or think about the word that was heard, which was very devastating. It's also a great blow to anyone in a similar thinking their marriage was going great when all along it was a big lie. I had to come clean and confess to her, that I was also seeing someone at the sometime.

It took a while for me to digest the words "I do not love you anymore." And that I am seeing someone that you know, after so many years in a marriage, how do begin to decode this message or even try to understand where the marriage started falling apart.

It was a very dark day, as the words kept reoccurring in my mind sounding like an echo in a cave "I do not love you anymore." I became angry, but not violent to the point of hurting anyone, just myself for not seeing the signs, how could it be when no signs of our marriage was falling apart, except that we were not intimate anymore the only problem was we slept on the side of the bed without touching each other, but we were civil to each other no matter what was happening at the time, was it there for some time, and paid no attention to it.

The big test we now faced was telling the children what has just transpired, and they may be a major change in their lives, which would affect them in all aspects of their childhood, into adulthood. The children were called to the den, by the looks on Dawn's face she sensed something was wrong, but did not know how bad it was. I had the job of explaining to Dawn, and Matthew, what had just happen to their mother and me, there would be changes with living arrangements, the looks in the children eyes, tears running down Dawn's face and the intense look on Matthew face said it all.

I did not want to up root the children from the house they both grew up in, or move them from the school they attended since early childhood, their mother insist she would take them to live with her. Although some resistance were made by both children it was my job to make them understand what needs to be done for all involve getting along, now that things were in the open with Sarah.

The children was not happy with the decision made, but had no choice who they should live with, but they agreed that they will live with their mother. The house was put up for sale, and was a complete shock to the neighbours, and our close friends when they drove by, and saw the for sale sign on the front lawn. We had to answer a lot of question, why we were moving? Did I get transferred to another city or another position at work? My answer to all their questions was simple no! Our marriage came to an abrupt halt, a decision that came about by some unforeseen circumstances, and left it at that.

At this time Didi never crossed my mind, having other problems to sort out was more important to consider, until everything is settled with the whole separation and divorce. The house was sold within three weeks of moving, I now lived in a town house, the children lived with their mother and continue attending the same school until the end of the school year.

It was very heart breaking for me at first, not hearing the children laughter or teasing each other was not music to my ears, things were very different now, with no noise in the house it was a lonely time of my life. After a long separation, and knowing our marriage could not be reconciled, the divorce proceedings began in the family Court, it was not a long proceeding, but time consuming, and wanted what was best for the children.

We decide that the children spend two weekends a month with me and they can call or see me whenever they want and I the same but their primary home is with their mother, with that problem settled and agreed on they were no more arguments. The courts had to put this down in writing and made sure it was going to be joint custody, that the children spend time with me whenever they feel the need to although they lived with their mother.

The separation lasted a year, before the divorce began, the friends or so called married friends sort of disappeared, and for some reason did not know why? The only thought coming to me was, they were afraid our divorce might rub off on them, hard to believe what your friends thought of you, now that you were not a couple anymore. After dividing what we had possessed over the years, we did not say much to each other, the hurt was still real, the only communication we had was about the children, and what were their needs?

A few week after the court granted our divorce they was another court hearing, this time it was for child support, at this point I was angry, my ex-wife wanted more money for child support although I had decided to pay for their expenses. The day of the court our names were called in the matter of Mr Andrew Fermin versus Sarah Fermin please comes forward to be heard.

She was not satisfied with the amount that we had agreed on so the judge had to calculate the amount that should be allocated for child support. The amount set by the judge was far less than what I had being paying all along for the support of both children, my ex-wife was very angry with the judge's decision, and tried to make me look bad, after the decision was handed down to her, all the necessary papers were signed and the case was over.

Over the course of a couple weeks she filed a complaint against me stating that I had abused our daughter, which was a lie, which was verified by our daughter that no abuse ever took placed, this whole court experience for me was a frightening one, on the whole I hate court, the idea of facing a judge was not something I ever wanted to do anytime soon again in my life.

All the time I was going through the separation and divorce myself and Didi, hardly spoke to each other, J did not want her name to be dragged through the courts and have Sarah finding out about us, was there a concern about the situation? yes it was! It was more to protect Alex and not have him tangled in the web that would have or may have hurt him in some way, if the lawyer she hired had any evidence that I was having an affair with someone from my Chicago office.

The least my ex-wife lawyer knew the better, after a couple of months had passed I called Didi informing her what had taken place with my marriage, and all I heard was "I am very sorry" that is ok, was my reply, I just wanted to know if you are ok and how was Alex doing. While talking to her his voice was heard in the background, and asked to speak with him. He was quite polite, and sounded all grown up the last time we spoke.

After speaking to him he said bye, and handed the phone over to his mother. We spoke for a while without bringing up any questions about the divorce, then she asked would they be a visit to Chicago soon, my reply was I do not know, but would try to get there soon. We said good bye then hung up the phone, after resting the receiver down, I realized that as much as I would like to see Didi, they was some sorting out of my life that took priority. They were so much to be done and lots of thinking now that singleness was here again.

I felt as though my marriage and as a husband and father was a failure, and should have fought harder to make our marriage worked, although I tried before the divorce, my ex-wife would have no part of it she simple was not happy, and wanted out of the marriage. After the divorced was finalized by the court my one priority in life was to get myself on track, although the kids came over to spend time with me it was not the same, it was not a family unit anymore.

The children went where ever I was going on the weekends, they were with me, they saw as many places, and got to know people in the towns we visited. My ex-wife was very snooty at times with me whenever the children came home late, on Sunday's right after they had supper.

I heard about a support group at a church, and made a phone call to one of the group leaders, and told her of my situation, and was told it was for the divorced, and separated, and meetings were held every Tuesdays of the month. The meeting day came and went and never gave an appearance, thinking to myself that it was not for me, and did not want to be seen with a bunch of divorced and separated people.

After three months of trying to decide if to go or not my decision was made so as the Tuesday came off I went and must say it was an evening never to be forgotten, and the greeting you got when you entered the room, when the meeting started everyone had to say something about themselves but when it was my turn, little was said at all. One of the group leaders said if you had nothing to say that was okay, for the rest of the night I sat and listening to what was said and the speech that night.

It took me three meetings to actually say something about myself, and the best part of talking was getting things off my chest, by listening to what other people in the same situation was talking about, and here thinking my situation was bad, in fact mine was relatively mild compared to the others that were in the meeting, and what they went through with their ex- spouses.

It later came to me in order to get better, and come to the realization of what happened in my marriage I had to overcome the results of the divorce, and all the court cases was part of my life and it was time to take charge of it, and start thinking in a positive way.

For the next several months that were ahead of me, the support group did lots of outdoors activities like hiking, baseball, walking, and camping. On many occasions they were open houses at myhome, and other members did the same. They were always quite a large crowd bringing snacks, food, salads, and a variety of dishes we all enjoyed while sitting, talking, and listening to some some soft quiet music with an upbeat tempo.

More positive things happened as the years came, I found myself doing lots more going to dances and picnic's they was something that I never did before live little theatre and the more plays I attended the more it became a joy to see, most of the time were comedy's where we could laugh, and not be stiff neck looking, all those who went to the various activities said they had a wonderful time, not for any moment with I was Involved with the divorce did I thought of my ex-wife (Sarah) which was a good thing meaning it was a sign of moving on and not dwelling on the marriage.

They were many parties to attend, and made lots of friends both male and female, but did not get involved with anyone, because of the soft spot for Didi, and did not want to do anything to hurt that relationship which was formed already. Yes they were some women that wanted to go out with me I did but, nothing came of it, deep down inside me the time was not right, to have any serious relationship or give anyone a commitment.

My healing journey had just began, and at this point the time was not right, getting into a real serious relationship with anyone although they were many female friends in my life they were l treated on a friendship basis. One of the things I remembered was taking a young lady dancing, New Year's night, not knowing how things would turn out, we went anyway and many of my friends were there, she was introduced to them l, and had such a wonderful time we decide to see each other from time to time, she was just separated and a single mother, and had no idea how long we were going to see each other.

Although we visited each other quite often it did not look as though anything would happen to that relationship, we came to the conclusion to remain friends. Time past, and for a long while decided to do my own thing, by myself, the time spent alone was quite busy doing interested thing that were being put off needing to be done, I began sketching, old buildings people, and making new friends along the way.

At one of the meetings a gentle lady asked me to help her with a program, she was running not knowing what it was about said yes! When the day of the class came I realized that the class was about separated and divorced which yours truly was one not that it felt shame to be in that bracket, fortunately for me this was a good option of actually participating, and learning from what others were saying about themselves, and listening to what this lady (Mary), which was her name was talking about.

Mary talked about letting go of all that intense feeling you had, and be yourself, for some time now after each session my mind was focused on the person I had shared a lot with, and began calling and talking to her on some occasions keeping in touch and asking how they were both doing. I did not make many frequent visits to Chicago as in the past, because of my promotion to higher position in the company, so was Didi, but at least we kept in touch every so often, she always asked, when and if they were any chance of me coming to Chicago soon.

It was not my intention to visit Chicago, but since she kept asking me about visiting, made up my mind to do so, it was a bright sunny day and made plans to visit Chicago, paying her a surprise visit, off I went on my arrival called the apartment, and Alex answered the phone, spoke for a while, in the background Didi's voice called out to him, asking who are you talking to, he replied! Your friend Drew, as she said hello! That soft voice brought back memories again, telling her where I am, she said! Stay right there we will be right over, and then she hung up the phone.

Standing on the platform at the airport and feeling anxious not knowing how things would turn out had me thinking, and seeing the car approaching my heart skipped a couple beats, it came to a stop, and out she came and for a moment did not know how to greet her but she knew came toward me with her arms wide open as if to say welcome back, greeted me with a big hug, and a kiss, as though nothing had stop in the time we had not seen each other. If felt great and was kind of confused not knowing how to respond to that greeting the choice was clear it was my turn to respond and that I did with a big hug and a kiss that lasted for a while and eyes gazing as we embraced each other.

Sitting in the car was Alex watching all that was happening outside, and between his mother and me entering the car he said hello, and asked how was my trip, it was good to see them again and it felt like old times, but in a sense for me it seemed as though it was a point of starting all over where we had left off a long time ago.

As we drove to her apartment the surroundings became familiar to me once again these were places we frequently visited whenever I came to Chicago. When asked the question, how long would you be staying? my answer was no more than a couple days, to me it was a surprise to her, because she wanted me to stay for a while so that they can talk and see where they both stood with each other, that was fine by me but, we both had things on our mind that needed to be said to each other.

We pulled up to the apartment drive way and Didi parked in the spot reserved for her, walking into the lobby she held unto my arms, as though it said welcome home, giving me a sense belonging, after all my marriage was on the verge of being over, and it was the perfect time for her to hold on to the person who was the father of her son. Alex who was now seven years of age and had grown quite a bit leading the way towards the elevator turned, looked at me and asked if he had seen his father lately.

Approaching the door of the apartment he stopped, turned around smile, and said! Glad you are here, well thank you! glad to be back, he held my hand gave it a gentle squeeze then proceeded to the door, he asked if he can open the door to show me he can, and what he had accomplished while I was away. He wanted to show me so many things he got before I sat down, resting my bag on the floor went to his room, and began talking about the stuff he received.

While Alex and I were talking Didi was in the kitchen preparing something to eat, she was called out, and said supper was ready, and we should come now before it gets cold, we all sat down and had supper, after supper had a choice of coffee, tea or hot chocolate while sitting at the table chatting with one another, Alex had finished his drink, asked to be excused, said he was going to his room and watched a show on television, Didi and I sat discussing the matter of telling Alex who was his father so he would have peace.

We cleaned the table, did the dishes; I washed the dishes while she dried and put them in their respectable places. We talked about the best time and place he should be told who his father was really. We had no clue what his reactions would be, when we both tell him that I was his father, would he be angry? Or would he be glad? The answer to the question, and his reaction we had no answer and what we should expect.

After Alex had finished watching his show Didi, called him out into the living room, he sat on the chair and both of us sat on the couch,

Alex, yes he replied your mom and I have something to tell you about your dad, and we find you are of age to know who he is we like you to meet him. He opened his eyes as wide as he can and shouted really! Yes we do, and as we were about to tell him the phone rang. It was Didi's mother she wanted to say goodnight to both of them. After talking for about twenty minutes she said goodbye.

While Didi was talking to her mother my focus was on how I am going to tell Alex his father was me, would he take it and smile or jump for joy knowing his dad was sitting in front of him, she came and sat on the couch, as we proceed to tell him Didi, started to tear up, she was now in a position to tell him who his father was, they would be many questions needing answers, we were sure about that but then again it may not happen until he absorb all what we were going to say to him tonight.

It was something the both of us were dreading for a couple years now, but the time has arrived that he should be told. He looked at both of us in a stunned way, and asked what is it that you have to talk to me about? We started to tell him about what had happened between his mother and me before he was born, and yes we loved each other then and still after all these years, but because of you we are still very close to each other, Alex we have a surprise for you, could you remember when you asked me if I knew your dad, and I told you yes, ah ha, well you are looking at him, he looked me in the eye and said no it cannot be then he asked his mother and she told him yes he is your father.

Alex, left the room very quietly and preceded to his room closed the door and with a loud shout thank you God for my father, after a while in his room he came out, sat next to me and with a smile, gave me a big hug said in his rather gentle voice Dad! Are you really my dad and do I call you dad from now on, yes if that is how you want to call me. For a moment there we both thought he would reject me knowing how much he had long to meet his father he was jubilant all this time I spent with him and his mother he thought we were best friends. He had lots of questions he wanted to ask us, but it was getting late, and a little past his bed time and said after school we would discuss everything informing you on some other things you need to know.

He got up bright and early the next morning, did everything he was told, and wanted to know more about me, but we had already told him after school, he looked at me several times with a smile, dad! He said can I hug you sure I replied, and another thing can you come with me when mom is taking me to school, well how can that question be refused, after breakfast got dressed and we l left the apartment, at this time Didi was watching every move Alex made, and was curious to hear what he would say when he opened his mouth to ask a question.

Alex and I got dropped off, and we walked up the side walk leading up to the front door of his school, some of his friends were walking behind, and he turned around and said to them this is my dad, your dad! Said one of his friend's yes! He replied, and he is staying with us for a while, the school bell rang and he went inside, and turning around walked pass the flag pole, hailed a taxi, and went to the mall, Didi had left both of us and went to work.

It was a beautiful morning; in Chicago at Didi's apartment t which was situated just outside the city amongst a beautiful park, surrounded with trees, the air was crisp, and fresh, with the sun shining through the branches and that cool breeze rustling through the trees as the leaves fell one by one. It was something that was never seen in California, where the leaves changed colours, it was a beautiful sight, with the falling leaves you knew, it was the fall season when you have to prepare yourself for those cold winter months that lies ahead of you.

Most of the day my mind ran on the things that Alex should know, and was not going to hold anything back what he does not ask would not be revealed, but it is good for him to know as much as possible not so much to overwhelm him at this point, the day seemed longer than usual maybe it is because I was not there to work, looking at my watch it was just about time for school to be over but had to wait on Didi, since he attends the after school program with other children whose parents are also working late.

Didi drove past me as I was walking back to the school since it was not far from the mall, and a little exercise could not hurt, she parked the car and walked towards me, held my hand, squeezed it and gave me a kiss on the cheeks, walking towards the after school program door, looking through the window was Alex, he was waving at us so he could be acknowledged we saw him, entering the class room he came towards us gave us a hug and said to the attendant this is my dad, I felt very proud of him an honoured to be his dad.

As we walked out the door he held our hands, and for the first time after my divorce the sense of it brought me back having a family, all over again, Didi looked at me and I did the same while Alex looked up at us. It was so good to see how happy he was knowing he had a father and can now relate to the rest of his school friends about having a dad, driving home all was a bit quiet until we turned into the entrance of the apartment, the excitement of him being home was overwhelming knowing they are some things we had to talk about.

He could not wait to get the elevator he ran in front push the button for his floor before we got there in side he held my hand and for the first time had the happiest look on his face it was a new experience for him and you can tell by his expressions he was thrill to have a father figure in his life. We entered the apartment and relax, while he had a small snack, then settled down doing his school work without asking any questions, after supper was served and the kitchen cleaned we sat and talked, while his mother looked at us having a conversation.

Didi did not say much while Alex and I talked but from time to time he would watch to see what she was doing, it made me think about what I was going to say in a manner he would understand. I told him he had two other siblings they were his half sister and brother, which he wanted to know about I told him Dawn was his big sister and Matthew his big brother, and shouted can I meet then, sure was my reply, first they would have to be told, they have a younger brother.

It was quite a joyous evening with both Didi, and Alex the questions kept coming as though they would never stop, one of the questions he asked was if Didi and I would get married, she looked at him then me, and with a gentle voice said Alex! That is not a question you should me asking right now, he looked at her and said, but I need to know, he then sat there thinking about another question to ask but could not come up with any at that moment.

His mother looked over at me nodded her head, and said yes! Drew what about that question are you going to answer it, that is something that have to be though out, but will surely get back to you as soon as the children is told about Alex, and you in the mean time let me say the chances looks promising, that is if you would have me as your husband.

Alex jumped up on his feet pulled his right elbow to his waist said an emphatic yes! His mother watched him with the gesture and started smiling, for a seven year old he asked a great amount of questions, and knew exactly what he wanted to asked, without any prompting, as though he had these questions entirely aligned in his head just waiting to ask them, he could not wait to hear what his two other siblings had to say about them having a brother, and was anxious he wanted me to call them so he could talked to them, but we had to tell him is was not a good time.

For the next couple days I had left, before returning to California we had a good time going about everywhere as a family which made me happy, since my family was broken up, and I saw what Alex and Didi bring to my life once more it feels good to be wanted. It felt as though I was back the way things were, once again that magical feeling we both had began to ignite, setting off some sparks which could be only quenched in the bedroom, when it was time for Alex to get ready we went into his room tucked him in and looking up at us and said good night mom, and dad, my heart skipped a beat hearing those words again.

Alex was now settled in bed and after having a tea, we went into the bedroom getting under the sheets the sparks began to fly and the passion and ecstasy came back as though it was yesterday, without missing a beat we were all over each other making love as though it was our first time, it felt good to have her back in my life wanting no else, our passion and love making went on for long time when it was over we were wet, with perspiration dripping down from our bodies as though rain was falling.

We went into the shower together cleaned up and at this point simple allowed the water to poured over us, enjoying every bit of being together. For the first time in a long time I began having stronger feelings for her more than before, and a deeper respect for her, because of who she is and what she has done for Alex while being absent as a father to him. I made a promise to her saying I would be always be there for both of you no matter how far I was, after drying off we got dresses and walked towards the bed she falling asleep in my arms while lying on my chest.

It was a beautiful finish to the day, and must say that the night sleep was peaceful for both of us, next morning there were no knocks at the door, but head the water running in the bathroom, and soon after the clinging of a dish and spoon knew exactly what he was having for breakfast.

After getting out of bed both Didi and I went to the kitchen for breakfast, Alex was still having cereal, milk and toast; he was enjoying his breakfast, because he said nothing until he had finished chewing whatever was in his mouth before saying good morning to us. It was Friday the last day of school, he left the table placed his dishes into the sink then off to his room to get ready.

He was so well trained by his mother that he knew exactly what had to done in order to get himself ready for school, Didi made his lunch, but told her today being Friday I would bring him a special lunch at school. She agreed not to make one when he came out I told him I would bring him lunch and asked what he would like, well let me think, oh yes some chicken strips, fries and a small orange juice, that is it, ok will get it to you at lunch time and may just have lunch with you today.

Didi, got dressed for work, while I cleaned and washed the dishes, and gave me a kiss Alex gave me a hug saying do not forget my lunch, which I simply replied I would not, out the door both went and continued doing the dishes, after cleaning and putting away the dishes, had a shave, showered, relaxed, and watched the local news. Since it was still early and had nothing else doing for a while, before taking Alex his lunch, they were no point in staying home, called Didi, to let her know I was going out to the mall, a taxi was at the door when I went down, which I did not called for.

Entering the cab, I told the driver where I wanted to go, and within about fifteen minutes he reached the mall drop me off. For the next couple hours did some window shopping looking to see what the coming fall fashion was about, before I knew it was approaching Alex lunch time, bought him what he had asked for and bought myself something so we can sit and have lunch together. The bell had just rang when I arrived, and went straight to his class to find him, when he saw me ran straight towards me with a big smile on his face.

We sat and had lunch chatting about his morning at school, and other questions that came up but nothing important that he was not clear about, he was just happy that we had a chance to sit and talk with out his mother being there it was us guys by ourselves, it was a good day knowing that I was having lunch with him brought such a wonderful and pleasant smile to him.

After lunch, I returned to the mall, shopping at some stores I had not visited especially the book store to buy some reading materials. It seems forever to me it seemed that the afternoon did not want to end, as the sun began to sinked lower into the horizon you could feel the cool breeze, and that it was going to be a cool evening, making a call to Didi, told her where I was, that she did not have to pick me up, because I was on my way home.

The taxi came as directed and after dropping me off came upstairs sat for a while, before deciding what to make for supper, they were two choices takeout or prepare supper making supper was the best choice. At 5:30pm the door opened, Didi, and Alex stepped into the apartment, greeted her with a kiss, and hugs them both, soon after the phone rang, it was Didi's mother. They both talked for a while and told her mother I was at her and had something to tell her tomorrow, so I promised to visit her Saturday after lunch.

We had a good home made supper, and talked about the day we had at work and school, Alex could not wait to talked about his day she allowed him to talked first, then it was her turn, after talking the dishes were cleared off the table, the washing of the dishes was done by me, Didi dried and put them away. All three of us sat and watch a show on television before the evening news came on. Alex in the mean time was in his room, he did not like watching the news, both of us sat and relaxed, holding hands while the news was on.

It was a mutual feeling we both had while watching the news, and for a brief moment thought about what, we were missing all along. My thoughts went back a couple years while attending university, she was in her first year and me my third year, with one more year to go, we dated for a long time even after graduating. We saw each other mostly on Friday nights, due to essay's she to prepare, along with her studies, papers that were due which had to be handed in on time.

It seems as though we were dating all over again, this time we had a son in the mix, which was good knowing she could not had asked for a better father for her son, she had a crush on me the day she first saw me, but could not tell me. It was one of her dorm friends that approached me about her wishing to meet me and ever since, the chemistry was there and still is in spite of me marrying someone else.

All these memories are still in the back of my mind, and in spite of it there are things so vivid to me now it could not be easily forgotten. They were times when we had to stay overnight at my apartment after one of our many dates, because of heavy rain. We sat and talk for hours until it stopped raining, when we walked out of the apartment she kiss me and said thanks for sharing, and told her the same.

Here we are again talking and sharing in her apartment instead of mine, suddenly a voice called out are you finished with supper, which brought me back to reality, and my reply was almost just a couple minutes, it was s good thing that Didi called out because I could have burnt the food being prepared for supper. At the same time the food was being prepared all the things that happened before my marriage, and during my marriage began coming into focus how Didi and I got back together all these years after graduating from university.

After supper was ready we sat down to eat, no one talked while eating the only words were, good stuff, pleased with myself I tapped my back, after supper we had ice-cream and cake for dessert, and relaxed for a bit before the news came on. Alex said he would clear the table, which he did, and I washed the dishes as usual, while Didi dried and put them away it was done as a family something that was never done in my past marriage.

The news came on just as we were finish cleaning and putting away the dishes. We both sat down to watch it. Alex went to his room to play, and came out after it was done. He sat between us and asked what we were doing tomorrow, so I asked what he would like to do, he replied go to the movies, but remember we have to visit your grandmother, yes! I know but we can all go to the movies after we visit.

We played a couple game of cards after turning off the television, and between his mother and Alex they played a game I never heard of it was a made up sort of a game they conjured up right there amongst themselves. I was beaten badly in most of the games played but learned that family have fun when they play together. I was very happy while doing so with them, we settled for a cup of tea Alex said good night to us, tomorrow been Saturday Didi and myself stayed up a little later before going to bed.

Surprising to say Didi was not very sleepy, and rest her head on my chest. She began rubbing it and felt relaxed. She started humming one of the many tunes we danced on many occasions. I responded with rubbing her shoulders and her hair but it sent a mild chill, up her back, and covered for a while but, started to get a little hot, shucked the covers off. She had on a short night shirt; suddenly she took it off and stayed in her underwear, while I had on pyjama without the top.

It was a quiet moment as we said nothing to each other then began rubbing herself over my body as if to say I am getting horny, and was in a mood for having sex. At this point everything she did told me t she was moving in that direction, taking of the bottom part of my pyjamas and she her underwear we started to get into that sexual mood where we felt the adrenaline rush coming into play.

It did not take long before we were in each other's arms, hugging, and kissing then all hell broke loose with the sexual drive coming into play. We got right into it she holding my penis, and placing it into her vagina, and the pleasures of the up and down action taking place with a sudden clawing to my back she let out a soft giggle and knew then she had an orgasm, and soon after my time came and gust of juice entered her vagina, we sigh and relaxed before cleaning up then we were off to bed.

Morning came as though we did not sleep, but we heard the sound of feet running in the hall way. We had no other choice but to get up and get ready to prepare breakfast. It was Saturday morning and did not know exactly what their weekend special was. I heard Alex saying breakfast is ready. We entered the kitchen, and there on the table was toast milk and cereal all set on the table, he smiled and said did I do well? We said yes! We sat down to breakfast, and after we had finished placed the dishes in the sink to soak Alex went and took his shower, changed his clothes because we were going over to his grandparents house to see her as promised.

Didi and I got ready, and before leaving called her mother letting her know we were on our way and if she wants us to pick up anything she needs, but she said no! So we left right after she drove, but made a stop at the road side market to pick up some fruits, and vegetables which was still in season.

Leaving the house, and watching Didi's face she looked as though something was on her mind. The only thing that ran across my mind was, she did not tell her mother who was Alex father, and to me it was the only thing thought about, when asked what she was thinking, she simple said she wanted to tell her mother a long time ago that Alex was my son. I could not tell her before telling Alex; now that she has told him it was playing on her mind the situation was right to tell her mother.

Because she was distant in her thoughts, asked me to drive so she can concentrate on how, and what she would say to her parents. The drive seemed to take a little longer than usual, I drove slow so she can have more time to think about her upcoming meeting with her parents, no sooner we pulled up into the drive way, even before the car came to a complete stop, Alex opened the door and ran to the door, rang the bell, and her parents came to the front door, surprisingly he did not shout out my dad is here. We entered the house her mother looked at her face, and immediately knew something was bothering her when asked what was on her mind she told them to have a seat.

The words took a long time to come out of her mouth but she finally told them that I was Alex father, and her mother replied how wonderful, she went on to explained that she did not tell them all these years because she wanted to tell Alex when he was old enough to understand why his father was not living with us. It took them by surprise but understood the complications it would have brought on him if she had told them before telling her son.

Alex was glad to know his father met his grandparents knew his father, we talked they asked me how things were and I told them good, and what was going to happen now that Alex knew who his dad was. It felt relaxed knowing everything was in the open; Didi explained her parent's how we met and what had taken place between us, the moment she found out she was pregnant with her son. She told her mother I was the only person she had ever dated, and went out with.

It was a relief knowing she did not dated or went out with anyone but I, all along my thought was on how sure was I about Alex being my son, and the idea of having a DNA test done to prove that Alex was my son, hearing what Didi said! Put my mind at ease.

It was good to clear the air with all the information that was held back about me being Alex's father and now it is known we can move forward to where we want to go from here. They were lots of talking today, and it set the mood for lots more discussions between Didi and me, where do we want our relationship to go. It gave way to some heavy thinking on my part, and again deep down in my mind asked myself this question am I ready to be part of a family again or do I want to stay single, and doing whatever I want without anyone permission.

What it all boils down to is me giving a commitment, which at this point in my thinking though it seems fitting the timing is wrong. It is not that my love for Didi is not true, but I needed a little more time to really figure things out. I am not saying that it scares me to give a commitment at this point but there are discussions I have to be talked over with my two children, when the discussion are completed then I would be in a better position saying yes to a long term commitment.

We spend most of the midmorning and afternoon with her parents, and Alex asked if he could stay over and be picked up later, Didi said yes, after saying our good bye we left for the mall to do a little shopping, driving along they were a big sigh of relief from her, after keeping this secret from her parents for years. It was a good feeling she said after sighing, it was good knowing that she was relieved of the burden after all these years.

Now that all the secrets were in the open she felt that she can face anyone, and anything no matter what, we pulled into the mall entrance parked the car and walked into the mall with her hand holding unto my arm, this was the first time in public she had done this, and it was good to know she still cares. They were no doubt in my mind whatsoever, there comes along one person who was meant for you some way along the road of life but it may take so many tries.

I thank God all the time I was able to have Didi as a friend first, and a lover now, not only as a good friend, but a stronger relationship that may turn out better than my ex-spouse. It has to be the right moment when we can say to each other it is time for us to be more than what we are now. We hope the day would come when we can be a family, and raise our son my other two children together.

We did not think about anything more than two people holding hands walking in the mall window shopping It was nice to hear her ask me about an outfit that she had liked, she went in tried it, and was a perfect fit, but was not quite sure about the colour. She picked out a top to go along with a skirt at home. It did not take long for the two of us to walk the mall, but decided to sit and sip either coffee or tea; along with a piece of apple pie or a donut either way we were going to have it.

Just as we were about to sit down a friend of Didi's saw her and came over to say hi! She introduced me as Alex's father and in a pleasant voice said hello. She and Didi left me sitting them both took off to a store not too far from the cafe where we were having tea that was fine with me because women like to chat about what they were going to buy. It was good for her to go with her friend. After she left I sat and read the newspaper, without realizing the time, it did not fizzled me she was gone for more than two hours, but this gave me some time to myself, thinking about what Didi means to me at this moment in my life.

They returned after completing three hours of shopping, and said she was a bit hungry, after saying good bye we left the mall, and went over to our favourite restaurant. In between eating she got a call from Alex asking what time we were picking him up and told him she did not know. He also wanted to know if he can spend the night, and told he ok but we will have to pick you up before noon tomorrow which was Sunday, he wanted to know why, and she told him that your father is going home. She ended the call after it was settled he was going to sleep there tonight and we get him in the morning.

After our lunch, decided to go home since we had nothing else to do, which seemed fair. We entered the apartment, and dropping the parcels at the door, started taking her clothes off saying let's make the most of it. A line of clothing was scattered from the hall way straight into the bedroom, and found ourselves on the bed carousing each other until that ecstasy and passion along with the rush of adrenaline not long after. We were making love till we began sweating, this came as a surprise to me the dropping of clothes all along the way, and we made the most of it without leaving the bedroom until we were exhausted.

Finally we sat up in bed, and looked at each other, and said wow! Then headed straight to the bathroom had a long shower together. It was a pleasure having a shower with her. We held each other while under the shower as the water fell like rain drops on our heads and body. We remained there for a while since we had nowhere to go in a rush, Alex was over at his grandparents, and was staying overnight.

We sat talking about the things we wished could happen right at the moment, but it was only wishes. In the future we would have to make up our minds what we want to do with our lives, talking mostly about Alex, and how is he going to feel when I leave tomorrow for home, and may not see me for a long time, though it seems unfair to him, knowingly he has just found out who his is father, and is about go away.

I have given this a lot of thought and the one thing can be promised is no matter what happen I will be there for him. The fact remains the two children at home have to know they have a little brother, how well they accept the fact is left to be seen, given the circumstances, both have to be told in a gentle way, it may be difficult at first but it would take some time for both to come to terms with it.

It was getting close to supper time but had not quite made up our mind what we should prepare for supper. We looked at each other, and sigh at this point we did not want to cook anything so it was decided eating out would be best. It was Didi's turn to choose a restaurant where she would like to eat, and she choose a restaurant she always wanted to visit, it was a quaint one on a side street not very fancy but very cosy and friendly.

We were seated in a corner overlooking a small pond in the courtyard, which was very fitting for us; they were no one else in that corner. It was very private for us to talk, and laugh, looking at the menu they were a wide variety to choose from, but being this was our first time here we asked the waitress what was the best menu most popular with the patrons. We both placed our orders, and had a drink or two before our meal came. It did not take long before we started eating, the choice we made were very delicious. We savoured every part of it taking our time chewing slowly, letting our taste buds enjoy the succulent flavour.

We did not keep the time in mind since Alex was at his grandparents for the night, we sat and talked and knew this is what we wanted in our life. There were lots of questions that needed ironing out with the children and me. This is something that we both can say, getting accustom to the idea would surely be a wonderful thing providing the children are in favour.

The question is what we are going to do if they said it is not fair, and they do not want to give up their father to someone else, it is something that has to be talked in about simply terms they can understand. It cannot be rushed but would have to make up their minds, because from where I am sitting it would be a shame to renege on the chance of being happy again, with someone that really has the understanding and caring feeling of a family.

I can understand how Didi would feel, so would Alex, he may feel not wanted by his sister or brother. We cannot say for certain what would happen but it's good to hope both would agree to us becoming a family. We had just finished supper when some soft music began to play, they was an area where you can dance to the music of your choice. We got up when one of our favourite tunes was being played; we danced until we were ready to go home. I was glad Didi choose the restaurant, making it another avenue for us to frequent when I am in Chicago.

After paying the bill we walked hand in hand towards the car, she decided to sit in the passenger seat while I drove home since she drank wine, as she was feeling a bit tipsy. It was a very good evening well spent with someone you really cared about, and I would gladly do it all over again. It was past eleven o'clock when we arrived at the apartment, and she could not wait to get undressed, without saying a word came towards me put her arms around my neck and started to gyrate her body on mine.

This was an invitation for her to have sex, and we were in sync to get on with it. We walked straight to the bedroom laid on the bed and started the love making process, with the ecstasy and passion and the rush of adrenaline we got right into the sexual act. She held my penis and directed it into her vagina, before doing so rubbed it up and down the outside walls of her vagina before placing it inside her. The moment it was inside the action of the up and down movement began until the climax of the organism took placed, many times over until we were exhausted.

The more time spent with her the more it felt as though my life with her can become a reality, but they would be things to be worked out, what I am talking here about was my other two children, and much thought have to be given about them. It is not that I am putting them before my happiness. I do not have a clue what they are going to say about the matter, then again what really do they know about love, giving them credit they might say well dad if it is what you want then go for it, and if she makes you happy why not get married again.

All this was running through my mind as we got dressed after some passionate love making, with all this action behind us I started packing. I was leaving Chicago for home the next day. It would be sad leaving Alex and Didi again spending time with them really got me thinking about them being part of a family, and coming straight from me at this point in my life it is something that was always in the back of my mind ever since she told me Alex was our child.

After packing we sat down and chat, me asking questions about us, and what she thought about us getting married, the look in her eyes said it al. She did not even have to answer that question for me to know, she wanted this to happen when that time arrived. She may not know this but deep down inside me the answer she gave with her eyes send a sparkle of joy to my heart and with inner smile thinking to myself yes!

The time was getting later as we spoke about different topics, one was where are we going to live, if and when we do get married, this was a problem. We have families in the cities where we lived, and uprooting them would not be fair, knowing how close she was to her parents and Alex to his grandparent. They would be no way she can desert them at this point, it is something that had to be worked out not only with her, but me and my children would they want to move from the school where they are going now to a school in another state that would be the question whatever the answer I would definitely have to wait and see.

It was midnight before we turned into bed she lying on my chest my hand was on her back, and did not knew when we both fell asleep. It was great lying next to her in bed, which made it feel that is where I belong. At this point I would do anything possible to be by her side in the future how soon that would be I cannot say but would be something I was looking forward to in the next couple months or even within a year.

The morning came and so did the rain, and thunder, I have not heard in a long time, but it was a pleasure seeing the lightning strokes across the sky with its brilliant display along with the heavy peal of the thunder. We lay in bed enjoying each other's company waiting for the rain, and thunder to stop. At this point we thought of Alex and what was he doing as the rain continued to falling, it was a good thing my flight was a later in the afternoon and I did not have to rush and get ready for the airport.

We were about to prepare breakfast when the phone rang Didi answered it and a conversation started then she glanced at me, and whispered it is Alex, he call, to say good morning. I replied good morning son, tell your grandparents good morning for me also, Didi continued her conversation with him until breakfast was almost ready, then she said goodbye and told him as soon as the rain, and thunder was over we will come for him.

The rained stopped two hours after breakfast, the sun came out with all its radiance lighting up the sky making it a bright and sunny day. It was good to see the sun, and with the rain that fell thought the sun would never come out, and that I would be leaving in the rain for home. After cleaning up the dishes and getting ready to get Alex. The time was just about 11:45amand as we left the apartment and taking one look realized here was a place with memories of all three of us as the song says stand by me gives me a lot to consider about my relationship with Didi over the years.

We drove to her parent's house my day dreaming began and came to an end as we pulled into the drive way it seems as though it was a short drive but in fact it was half an hour, but longer on a work day since it was Sunday. They were less traffic on the road, we stopped the car and looking through the window was Alex, and came towards the door when he saw us getting out the car. We entered the house ran towards his mother and gave her a big hug, and gave me a high five saying good morning dad, then went and sat on the couch until we were ready to leave.

He asked me what time my plane was leaving, and said he had time to talk with me when we got home before being driven to the airport, which was nice of him. It was agreed when we got home we are going to talk telling you the truth. I do not have any idea what he want to talk about but would have to wait. We sat and talked to his grandparent for a good hour before leaving, his grandmother asked me when I was coming back, and I told her Didi would let her know of my return.

We all said goodbye to each other, and drove onto the road for home, because it was getting close to lunch, and hunger pangs were being felt we had a quick bite to eat at a small restaurant that sold burgers and wings. We had a helping of both dishes, then we left for home, in the apartment Alex asked me when I was going to see him again, and had to say sooner than you think because he was very much part of both of us it was hard to say that when the time permits me to travel.

We talked for an hour before the time came to leave for the airport, taking Didi into my arms we both exchanged kissed. Her face appeared sad, and had to ask her why the face, she said you are leaving just when I was getting accustom to having you around. I will miss you a great deal because over the last couple days I have gotten closer to you now than ever, all I can say is that is the way my feelings were for a while now, but kept it under wraps to myself but now that she know, it felt good hearing it from me, and hearing it from her lips.

As we left for the airport I looked around and a bit of a tear came to my eyes but did not let anyone see, and again that connection between Didi, Alex and me came into play. We drove to the airport, checking in my bags had some time to spend with them before the flight was announced, and it made me feel good as though I was on a trip to another state, and would be returning home after my work there. It seemed all too familiar because that was the way it was when I was married to Sarah, and had to leave for Chicago before returning home.

It was quite a while before my flight was announced and Alex wanted to walk around so we allowed him all the while watching his every move, although he did not wander far from out sight. We paid close attention always knowing where he was at every turn, sitting and chatting was not something that happened in my previous marriage. It was good they was someone in my life who wanted to sit and talk with me at the airport while I wait for my flight to be announced, sooner said the announcement came over the speakers and it was my queue to get ready, kissing Didi, and giving them both a hug said goodbye. I entered the gate for my flight, looking back the hands kept waving until it was no longer seen. The plane left on time, and before I knew what was happening it was up in the air the thought of saying goodbye felt like a sad day as though the bottom fell out of my heart. I know however we were going to see each other in a short time once again.

On the flight home the scenario was played out over and over what I had to tell the children, but as the time went on I kept changing the words I had to say to them. I realized the first thought entering my mind was the one that should be told. It was jotted down on a piece of paper along with some questions they may ask about Didi, and Alex after writing these questions down took a little nap knowing the flight was a long ways away before landing.

Between napping and waking the pilots voice announced we should be landing in about twenty minutes, my heart skipped a couple beats knowing I have to tell the children about Didi, and Alex. The fact is they had another sibling they need to know about something that may not sit right with them at first, but giving it time to comprehend in they may come around, and start asking questions about them both.

I did not give it any more thought again, as the plane touchdown on the tarmac it felt good to be home, but had all these answers to questions they may asked. I quickly got my bags, and proceeded straight for my car. I made a call to Dawn letting her know I just landed and would see them during the week, and had some things to tell them, although she was curious, no questions were asked, what it was all about said love you daddy! Good to have you home.

I finally got to my apartment and walked in sat down on the couch did not even looked at the mail on the center table, took my shoes off and relaxed for bit. I made a call to Didi letting her know that all is well and everything was okay, thanking her once again for the time we spent together. I had no regrets at all, knowing how I really felt about her was wonderful, and hope that it would continue with so much things we have to offer the children if we did get together.

I put the receiver down they was a knock on the door, and standing at the door was Matt, and a couple of his friends Hi dad, good to have you back, how did you know I was back? Dawn texted me, I wanted to see you because I miss you while you were gone. They came in, made themselves at home, anyone want something to drink, no they said we are not staying long we are off to the mall have to do a little shopping and some browsing, bye dad, and left but before he left told him I wanted to talk with both of them one day during the week, okay!.

After Matt and his friends left, my thought were on Didi, and Alex I could not help thinking how things would be like if all the children got together, sometime during the year after school was on holidays. I started preparing something to eat for supper; put the television on watched the news as supper was being prepared. It sure felt a bit lonely knowing a couple days ago I was sitting as a family, now it was back being just me. It is now sinking in my mind, just thinking, how it felt being part of a family again, knowing that feeling was there a couple days ago.

The football game was on I sat down to watched it and into the second half of the game I had a nap between that game, and the second one. The first game was sort of boring compared to the second one which had lots of smack talking and hard hitting, with the score even going into the second half. I did not take in much of the second half but changed channel to watch the news, and what was happening around the city.

The sun was just setting and the skyline was a beautiful array of different light displayed by the sun, and clouds as the evening progressed, one not seen in a long time oh what magnificent display of colours. The pleasure of just watching it wished someone special was here to share it with, am I thinking too far ahead of myself or am I wishing things were different in my marriage to Sarah. It was something that never crossed my mind in all these years but, now why all the reflection of what has gone and no longer is?

Reality was there all right now that my thinking was intact, and that part of my life was over it was now time for me to make a decision to face the fact that Didi, and Alex are now in my life, and losing them would be a mistake. They are lots to think about, and decisions to be made about where we would live and work, would I have to relocate closer, and would Didi and Alex move closer or relocate to

California where I live and work, can I make that move all within a year or two that was the questions now playing out in my mind along with me telling the children what my intentions are. Although they do not know about Didi, and Alex as yet, but very soon they would.

My concentration on the news was not they because of the many things that was playing out in my head so back to the football game, which was still in progress, it was use to deter me from thinking anything else so my focus was now on the game at hand, it was a good game one which brought me back to not trying to get myself all tangled up with too much thinking.

The games ended around 11:00 pm, and by this time my eyes began to close somewhat, and knew that it was time for bed, after washing the dishes and putting them away got myself ready for bed. The next day which was Monday it was back to work after a mini holiday. The morning seems too arrived earlier than usual, for some reason maybe I am still on holiday mode, after taking a shave, and shower had my breakfast in a blink of an eye I was on my way to the office.

On the way to work something strange caught my attention on a bill board which read “You are one in a million that would read this sign” what it was about, I had no clue what they were talking about. They were no pictures to show what it entailed, reaching the office building some staff members was standing outside looking up towards the roof, on the roof was a gentleman who was attempting to commit suicide by jumping, within ten minutes of getting there the fire truck, ambulance, and police arrived attempting to find out what the gentleman on the roof was about, where he came from and who was he.

It was an exciting morning, no one was allowed into the building. We stood outside for an hour, while the police and firemen prepared their safety nets, in case the man jumped. It so happened they called and ask him his name, he said James Burke, it sounded familiar, and then it came back to me, the gentleman once worked for us, and because of his tardiness he was released. At that point he asked for one of the department head he worked for, the time they made contact with that manager he jumped, in his hand he clutched a piece of paper which was blank.

It was a ghastly scene, which no one expected that morning. I had no choice but told everyone to take the day off because of the episode they witnessed. I stayed back, along with the manager of the department where the gentleman worked, his wife was called by the police, and within a couple of minutes a police officer brought her to identify him, he was pronounced dead at the scene but the coroner had to make sure he was indeed dead and notice the time of death, it certainly was a sad day on this beautiful morning.

After the parking lot was cleared of all the equipments used by the firemen, I made my way up to the office to see if they was any paper work that needed my attention right away, since they was no urgent work, needing my immediate attention, I did some work that was started, before leaving for Chicago, and said to myself while sitting at the desk, what a hell of a way to start the morning.

The drama that was played outside the office building was real, and I kept thinking about the gentleman for some time, and the effects it would have on his family, friends and, associates whoever they maybe. I did not know him personally but his name does come to mind now that I recall his behaviour was brought to my attention on many occasions. My work progress was not happening the way that it should turn out so after a couple hours packed up some paper work and proceeded home where I can best concentrate on it.

In the blink of an eye that is how fast things happened this morning, it was not that the equipment was not strong to protect him. He changed spots so fast they could not move around to where he had jumped, and that was the big difference, when he landed on the ground is a sad occurrence. It was within ten feet the firemen with the net missed him all together. I thought for sure they could have saved his life, for some reason he did not appeared he wanted to be saved at that point.

This was a day that should not be forgotten not by me or anyone who witnessed that fall at the scene, anyway life goes on work was something I had to focus on and not the event of the scene this morning. My other focus was my children about the details we have to discuss about Didi, and Alex, and all who are involved. I do not want them to feel left out in some decisions that was going to be made by me, in order to come to terms with what must be done I thought it was the best thing that can done for them and myself.

Along the way I made a stop at the groceries to get a few items, and ran into an old friend I have not seen for a long time. We talked then said bye to each other, we soon parted company, and in the distance walking by herself was Sarah, she did not notice me, but went my way it is not that we do not talk it is only when the children have a problem she would call, and talk, other times nothing, and that is the way I prefer it.

The way home for some reason seemed to take a bit longer why? I do not know but after getting home, relaxed for a while and work became my focus. I started without any interruptions which were good in a sense, with the quietness of the house, and not hearing voices talking, putting on the radio to a talk show was the only way the house was filled with voices with argument amount the guest and the hosts.

As the rest of the day progressed, so did my work but stopped at times to eat it did not feel like an office with paper work lying on the table in the kitchen. It was like a casual day having paper work done at home, but as the saying goes "do it with a smile on your face" in that way you would have everything finished in a jiffy which it did. I packed my work into my briefcase and started dinner, turned off the radio and put the television on the local news channel listening for the incident that took placed at the office parking lot, but there was none. I changed to another channel and, the whole incident was being played out again.

Tonight sports were Monday night football, and hope it would get my mind off the episode that happened in the parking lot at work. Before the game began I called Didi and when the phone rang that familiar voice answered. We talked for a while and the other voice in the background wanted to know who she was speaking too. I thought he was a bit curious to find out when she told him it was his father he immediately said, can I talk to him? Yes she replied but not for long, okay! He came on, and asked how I was, how was my day and, a lot of other questions one in particular, have I spoke to his sister and brother had to tell him no, but on Friday I would be talking to them.

He said bye! And gave the phone back to his mother, we talk about everything that happened during the day, which was good for us, and the time we spent talking it felt so comfortable not having suspicious feeling I had with Sarah, it was a joy talking to her. I know now what I saw and heard what she said to me in Chicago was all real. I have no doubt in my mind that if and when the time came it would be her I would settle down with, at this time of my life.

Without giving it anymore thought we talked for another hour before saying good night and love you to love each, and that in a way was strange because I have never heard it in a very long time. The last time that happened was in Chicago a couple weeks ago, but it different because I did not know how she felt about our relationship, but now it was a known fact she cared, we can both tell each other how we feel. After hanging up the phone I sat and watched the football game in its entirety, and was glad I did the game was full of hard hitting and fast pace running along with some high scoring. I went to bed a little after the game was over, made sure that the apartment was secured lights off then head to the bedroom.

I awoke around six o'clock in the morning to the sound of what I thought was a crash outside, it was only the garbage truck backfiring.

I stayed up, going back to bed the chance of me oversleeping was great, and it would not be a good thing. I went out collected the newspaper, sat for a while reading, and before I knew it the time to get ready for work was here. I had to hustle for a bit just to get ahead of the time.

After all the hustling made my breakfast, and was out the door, briefcase in hand, and proceeded towards the car. It was a much quieter morning than usual, the sound of noisy engines was far less, and people on the street were also less. The drive into work was very pleasant no traffic jams which was good for me, most days the traffic can be stressful, and can be bad for everyone due to the lack of courtesy with every one trying to get ahead of you, and would do anything no matter what it takes. The road rage is something you had to deal with when the traffic is heavy.

The parking lot at work was now cleaned up, and there were no signs of any commotion had ever taken place yesterday, parked the car in my usual spot and took a little longer getting to the main door of the building. I was trying to figure out how did the gentleman that jumped got on to the roof of the building, because there were guards on duty at all times in the front hallway. I cannot imagine what his wife and his entire family must be going through, the pain that they are in and l the turmoil he has cause on account of his selfish act, which leaved me thinking why he did not seek help if he needed it before the time of his demised.

I could not help wondering the what if's questions that is going through the minds of his relatives, and the predicament he has place on them not to mentioned the financial burden they have to bear. My thoughts was on the family, going through the elevator doors I thought the only way he could have gotten pass the guard was acting as though he was still employed here, but instead of going to a floor went straight up to the roof and stayed there till morning to carry his threat a promised made to himself. He may not have had the idea to jump but it seemed as though, may be he wanted to scare those of us on the ground. This we may never know since there was no writing on the paper clutched in his hand when he jumped, or whatever caused his death may be he was dizzy from the high.

We can only speculate, and give our opinion it is all we can do for now, to tell you the truth it is not for me to ask why? Or what he was thinking, that is between he and God. As the day progressed it was not hard to see, or hear what the talk was about in the office. It was good to know almost everyone was talking about the incident that took place yesterday, and they were coming to terms with it so they could move pass the issue, getting back to their normal work pattern.

The only thing that can be done at this point was to send flowers from the office and have a collection of funds to help his wife, who might be in a financial situation, this was done, some of the office workers decided to attend the funeral as soon as they knew the date and time. We settled down after the necessary itinerary for the financial arrangements were taken care of, and doing some work trying, to move pass yesterday's mishap.

I had a good morning after all, since the whole incident was behind me, most of my efforts were now focus on the next coming day of the week, but mostly on Friday when I can present the question about Didi, and Alex to my two children making them part of a family. I was not sure of the outcome but if the issues are not presented to them the answers would not be there. The afternoon was closing in very quickly and within a couple hours it would be time to go home, and relax from a hectic day.

The familiar sound was heard the shifting of chairs, the sound of drawers being closed, file cabinets and other office furniture being put away for the next morning, then it was time to get out and enjoy the fresh air. The workers started to file out one after the other to the elevator, along with other workers took the stairs which was twelve floors down, this was a good exercise which I needed having not done any since my return from Chicago.

The walk down took about ten minutes, and was glad to get into the fresh air the workers that came down with me said good bye and left in different direction for their home of whatever community or town they lived. The drive was a bit slow made a stop to pick up a few items that was needed. I did not ran into anyone, and was in and out the store in twenty minutes then proceeded home to get out of the rush hour traffic as fast as possible, home at last, all safe for another day. I collected the mail from my mail box entering the apartment closed the door behind me went straight for the couch to relax before making my supper, and looking at the evening news.

They were not much to watch after the news therefore, I settled for the newspaper, then a good book to read after supper, together with a glass of red wine to keep me company. I folded the newspaper after a couple pages, and made a call to Didi, and Alex but they was no answer, I can only guess she may be over at her mother's for a visit, placing the receiver down went back to reading. I have not read a book in a long time and found this one to be quite interested, which held my curiosity until it was time for bed.

The reading was something I have been putting off for quite some time and had no sought of interest in reading any books or newspaper since the news was interested to me and any educational programs then. Just after having finished the wine the phone rang three times before answering it, and to my surprise it was Didi, wanting to know how my day went after yesterday's incident. I told her it was a good day, and what we done for the family and some of the workers said they would attend the funeral when they knew some more of the particulars.

We talked for twenty minutes, in the background was the sound of Alex voice calling his mother about a question he had for home work, then he wanted to know out of curiosity who she was speaking to, when told he shouted say! Good night for me please, and that I would talk another time, Didi was a bit anxious, and wanted to know the best time to call me on the weekend after the children was told about us being a family some day.

After saying good night and good bye, I walked towards the sink wash and the dishes before going to bed. I was beginning to get sleepy, due to the wine I had while watching the news. Without giving it any thought proceeded to the bedroom changed in to my pyjamas did my night routine and rest my head gently on the pillow, a few minutes after turning out the lights, I to be a drag, and could not wait for the weekend to come, it was only the middle of the week, and they were a couple more days to work before the weekend. was sound asleep. The morning came, too soon, and the whole cycle of getting ready the same time each day was starting

With all that thinking the alarm went off telling me it was time to get moving if I want to get work on time. I picked up the pace completing my morning routine, I grabbed my briefcase and out the door, proceeded straight towards the car and off to work stopping briefly for a takeout breakfast my Wednesday morning routine which I started a while back as a treat to myself

My work day had just started when the phone rang; it was one of the departmental manager's that wanted to talk about something's with me so, down to the other floor to see him. It was a change of scenery it had been a long time ago I had visited that floor. It all seemed change now to when I was there last, furniture's and cubicles were arranged in a way it was easier to see everyone at any time, which was a good before going into the manager's office I said hello to most of the workers on the floor and had a few good conversations with them.

It gave me a chance to listen to what they wanted to project, it was good for them to voice some opinions about where the company is heading, after saying thank you and good day, and I went to the manager's office. We sat and had a conversation, from what he told me Monday's incident had a profound effect on him, and it brought back some memories of the past, because his brother had committed suicide, and he tried to deal with it the best way possible, just when he was getting through this happened and threw him in a downward spiral.

He wanted to let me know he might be taking a leave of absent for about a week to think about his unresolved issues and to see a counsellor about issue that was bothering him. It was all well, and good he came to terms with it as soon as he recognized the symptoms. I told him it would be ok, and should let human resources know about it, although we do have retained a counselling service he chose to get one he was comfortable with.

Returning to my desk after that conversation, the opinions of the staff on the third floor came back and jotting down some points that was said typed a letter to all the departmental managers based on those opinions we need to have a meeting sometime next week, so they can add any opinions they may have on the topics that we would be discussing.

The work day was going very smooth, without any problems, it was good to know that my paper work was now under control, and was free to talk to anyone at anytime during the day, that can all changed in a second, within a couple minutes the phone rang. It was Matt's school calling to inform me he had an accident at the gym while practicing basketball, and was being taken to the hospital for x-rays, which was the normal procedure when anyone got injured at school. The reason he called was he knew that I would understand what he was going through, because of a similar injury that occurred to me when I played.

The drive to the hospital was not far, but the traffic was terrible, the traffic light kept turning red for most of the way, entering the front door I went straight for the information booth, asked for Matt..........., and was given the directions where to go, seeing him was a sigh of relief. I knew he was ok, the doctor walked towards me said it was nothing serious, but a hairline crack, and they were going to put a cast on his ankle so that it would heal properly, after saying thanks they took him into a room. The cast took about an hour, he finally came out with crutches, and said lets go home.

The work week started on a bad note, and here I am at the hospital this has been the second incident that took place since this week began, it is said that things happens in three's so what can happened now before the week is completed was the question. I would have to wait and see, if that is true or just a myth, he walked to the car, and I dropped him off at his mother's home where he lived, told him good bye, I loved him and would see him on the Friday after work.

I did not returned to work instead went home because it was close to the end of the work day, parked the car, collected the mails, and went into the apartment, took my shoes off and relax on the couch. I laid my head on the cushion the phone rang, Matt wanted to know if it was ok to skip school tomorrow, but my answer was ask your mother, and hear what she has to say on that subject.

The rest of the evening was quiet with no other interruptions until close to my bed time then the phone rang, who can be calling at this time of the night. The only thing I could think of was another emergency to another one of the children, but it turned out Alex wanted to talk to me as promise. We talked for twenty minutes about his school, and how he was doing otherwise, he said good, ask me when he would see me, because he misses me now, and wish that I was there. My answer was as soon as possible after I talk to your sister, and brother I would call, and let you know when I am coming, after saying good night, he gave the phone over to his mother.

Her voice sound even sexier than usual, you can hear it in the tone of her voice. We talk for a while I did ask how she was doing right now, and she said she misses me and wish I was here with her, because it was starting to get colder, and wish she had a body next to hers to keep her warm My thinking was the same, but that would have to wait till I can get away.

The conversation between Didi, and me went on for a while longer since we did not get a chance to speak on Tuesday morning, we talked about everything we could think about, and as we spoke realized that our love for each other was getting stronger every day that we were apart, and our relationship was intact. If we are going to make it this was the test of all tests.

It was now way past her bedtime she said good night, and me the same then we hung up the receiver, before laying down sat up for a while thinking about the things we have to work out with the family on both sides, finally after lying down fell asleep. I woke up the next morning with a little more spunk in me because of the things we both talked about last night.

I was on cloud nine because of what Didi said to me, and for the entire day felt good about myself, and did not let anything interrupt my day. It was a very good day indeed, the start of a good workday with my mind set on work started where I left off the day before the hospital visit to get Matt, the day went by so fast that I paid no notice of the time, after looking at my watch it was almost close to the end of the workday, without any hesitation stayed over a bit longer. I had some paper work to signed given to me by my secretary before she left for home.

The day was coming to a close the sun was starting to set, and the glow and warmth of the sun was no longer there but the different colours magnificently displayed as the sun began getting lower. I left the office, drove to my favourite restaurant, and had supper knowing it would have been too late for me to prepare it, then sit and eat. I ordered my supper and it came promptly, and along with it a beer, watched whatever was on the television until supper was completely eaten. I got up to leave the restaurant, and someone from my past walked in, seeing me sitting alone sat at the table with me. We talked for almost an hour, and found out she told herself one day she was going to get me in bed with her somehow no matter what, soon after talking she left, what a surprise.

I had no indication that this woman had such a crush on me, when I heard what she said I had to say wow! She wanted to know if I was seeing anyone in town, what surprised me is as a married woman how in the world, is that going to happen since I did not want to sleep with her. This must be a woman that is fantasizing about a relationship with me thinking that it would happen someday.

The woman had me thinking, knowing that she was married why I would want to put my relationship with Didi in jeopardy for her, this to me was a test to really see if I would come unto her but that would never happen not now, finally home was in sight and after parking the car the woman drove up behind me, and ask if she can use the bathroom, I said bluntly now but since she only knew where the building was and not the apartment I pretended to go to another building letting her think that I was living there.

She left just when I was entering the building, so I retraced my steps and entered my own building entrance, gee what fast thinking, after entering my apartment I watched the 7:00pm news and had a glass of wine to relax before doing any reading. It would be ashamed for that woman to go to bed with a stranger, and end up dead, although I have never met her husband my thoughts were on him, does he know what his wife was up too, if at all, so without anymore thinking of her again my focus was now somewhere else, made a call to Didi, and Alex to find out how they were doing.

The call went through and that little voice answered oh hi dad, how are you? Fine was my reply, and what are you doing? Home work and mom is making sure it is completed before going to bed, have to go now love you dad, me too son then Didi came on hi! How was your day great she said good, no problems so far, not hoping for any, just had to call and tell you that I had a proposition put to me, and what was it, some woman I knew asked me to sleep with her, the nerve of that woman she said! What did you say in no uncertain terms is it ever going to happen?

The conversation was a pleasant one, and I asked her about Christmas, if she would like to visit California for a couple days over the holiday season, and it was not a surprise for me to hear her say yes, okay I said, but please do not tell Alex anything until I talked to Dawn, and Matt about it I would get back to you on that subject, after a few more munities we both say good bye and hang up the phone. It would be so nice to have her here with me, during the Christmas period, and that the children can finally meet her but that is a hurdle which have to be crossed.

The weekend was just approaching, and that means the children would have to decide what was going to take place after we spoke about Didi, and Alex about being part of the family, this would not be easy for them but at least they would hear what have to be said on that subject and would have to say whether it is something they think that they can have an open mind to the fact that Didi, and Alex are already part of the family in some way.

At last the weekend was here it is now Friday as the work day began to end, the office was buzzing what each person was going to do, whether it was partying or just relaxing with friends in the back yard. I had lots to look forward to this weekend, the phone rang just as my foot was out the office doorway, it was Matt, reminding me not to forget he was waiting at school for me, when asked about his sister said he have not seen her all day hoped you pass for her also.

Gathering my thoughts, and the questions I need to ask them seemed straight forward, and to the point, knowing them, they would also have questions for me. I arrived at school they were both waiting, and before I can say good evening how was your day at school, they both asked what we were having for supper. My suggestion was what would you like, and both said something good how about the family restaurant that you took us to many times before.

Driving to the restaurant they were a bit of silence, but it all ended when Dawn wanted to know what I had to discuss with them, so my answer was you will have to wait till we get home, she said that is ok. I cannot imagine what was going through her head that she was so eager to get to the discussion, and give me her opinion. She like to size up the situation before giving an answer, which was fair not that I was going to hear something negative but the way she would feel about things on the whole generally speaking.

All three of us sat down to supper, and talked about what ever subject came up, after our order was taken Dawn talked about her science project, and Matt about his best friend both having different opinions on the subject which was interested to hear them give each other feedback. It was though my presence was absent, so I listened to them before stepping in to say a couple words, just then our supper arrived and we sat in silently eating enjoying our meal.

After our meal both wanted something for dessert, she chose vanilla ice-cream, his were strawberry ice-cream, and I pistachio ice-cream along with carrot cake, when we were finished, the bill was paid and we went home. We picked up a few items at the grocery for the weekend along with a couple packages of snack for the nights while watching a movie or a show on the television.

The drive home was full of laughter and talking with both children trying to outdo each other at times, what I must say about them is they lookout for each other, and that is very good. We got home and it was a sort of rush between them to get the control for the television, knowing that they would try to get it before each other I moved it from its regular spot. They had to wait until I came in the house, put the few items away before handing the control to them.

They did not argue about who should get it but decided amount themselves what they were going to watch, for a moment. My thought were they had forgotten all about the talk we had to discuss, and from nowhere Dawn brought it up, so dad what is it that you want to talk to us about? with the television switched off the conversation started. It started about when I was in university I had dated this girl, she was in her first year, me in third year, we went out for a long time up until I got married to your mom. We lost touch with each other, and when the Chicago trips came up for me to visit our office there she was working at that office.

As time went on we became a little friendlier, and from time to time she would call to find out how I was going, although she did not know your mother. She would always ask about her, all this took place before anyone of you was born. We kept in touch over the years, and every time I visited the Chicago office she was always around, talking about different things, she was part of the problem solving team, and was always at meetings when they were held.

From time to time we had supper together, which lead to a sort of romantic interlude, we got too close to each other she got pregnant, although she was seeing someone else. She had a baby boy, and did not tell me anything until a few months before your mother, and I began to have difficulties with our marriage. While visiting the Chicago office on one occasion she wanted to talk to me about the baby she had, he was two years of age, since she wanted to talk I thought she wanted me to be his Godfather, not knowing anything about what she wanted to talk to me about agreed, when the chance came we sat and talked. What she told me was a big surprise, she said I was her son's father, and was glad it was me.

All this time I kept it a secret from you both, because this has been bothering me for quite a while I thought it was time for you two to hear what I had to say about the matter. This had nothing to do with your mom, and me getting a divorced at all things happened between your mother and me because she showed less love for me at times.

I brought the issue up because I want to hear your opinions, now that you know some of the details, do you have anything you wish to say, or do you want some time to talk it over with each other. We discuss it in the morning, if you like but there is another issue we have to talk about since your mother, and me were divorced I have not been seeing anyone. My last visit to Chicago encountered with a romantic episode with this person, her name is Didi, and her son name is Alex, and we talked about getting married. I told her before anything happens a discussion would have happen between you two to hear your opinion on the matter of me getting married again.

They both looked at me, and without any hesitation said dad if you are happy with this person we would not stop you as long you are comfortable with the idea, that was not the answer I had expected, but more of an open discussion on the topic. What really shocked me was the way both came to the conclusion it was ok to do what would make me happy, and if Didi make me happy go for it. I want to show you a picture of Didi, and Alex I showed them they picture, and they wanted to know how old he was, and when can they see them or talk to Alex.

My answer was soon, how do you feel about them coming here for Christmas for a few days, the answer I got from them was that would be great Dawn, and Matt had now accepted the fact they now have a little brother, and was now eager to see him. We laugh, and talked some more about the whole issue surrounding the topic at hand, and was looking forward to the next coming week. I breathe a sigh of relief now all the talk about Didi and Alex was out of the way we sat and watch television until bed time. We all said goodnight to each other and went to our separated rooms, I could hear both of them talking about the issue. They both said they were glad t dad found someone, and were very glad about the outcome, and I know they were genuine about me finding someone that I cared about.

The night seemed a bit longer for me, because it was difficult falling asleep, with all that we talked about, and what was going to happen in a couple weeks when Didi and Alex would be here for the Christmas Holidays. I was definitely looking forward to seeing them, sleep came and before I knew it morning came, and voices could be heard in the kitchen, as though they were talking on the phone to someone. I poked my head out the bedroom on the phone was Dawn talking, when asked who she was talking too, her answer was Alex. They were having a good talk with each other for a while them Matt talked to him the way boys would talked to each other, they now thought of him as a little brother they were looking for, and had just found all these years.

After they both talked to Alex, and Didi the phone was handed to me, hi she said, how you are doing, and how was the talk with the children. It went well considering what I thought would have been opposed quite a bit but both came to terms with the idea I was in a relationship with you, anyway how did they sound to you, good! Looks like you hit it off with them. They both agreed to have you both come here for Christmas holidays.

With that answer she said! Really yes! what day were you thinking of flying out here. I really do not have a date set but will get back to you when I talk to Alex about it, great I said, then we said love you to each other, and hang up the phone. The question was who wants what for breakfast, and all said the usual, which consists of bacon, eggs, home fries, and sausage with tea or coffee. I started preparing breakfast when Dawn approached me, and said dad, Didi, sounds nice I am looking forward to meet her, and Alex at Christmas thanks I said, and continued making breakfast, Matt did not say too much he was watching a show, and was caught up with whatever was going on the television at the time.

Breakfast was ready, and we sat down to eat when Matt started talking Alex sound good, and wish he was here so he could take him out to the mall, but knew he would have to wait until he come for a visit. After breakfast we took off for a drive and some hiking which we did from time to time, walking to our favourite place we sat, and enjoyed the view from where we were sitting, looking out we saw the cars as they drove along the freeway.

The time when fast walking back to the car we got hungry, and decided the restaurant where the truck drivers stop and ate. It was busy but was seated, and within a couple minutes the waitress came along with the men. We ordered burgers, fries and shakes talked for a while before our orders came, it was good to see them laugh and carry on a conversation, with all they were told they embraced it without any problems. The food came and we all finished together remaining there for a while watched the truckers as they came in to have something to eat, what they ate was no surprise to me. They ordered two hamburgers each with a large fries, and the biggest mug of cola they could drink.

I paid the bill, and left a tip then we walked out got into the car and head for home, on the way they wanted to visit the mall so we stop. They both went separated way to shop, while I sat in the food court with a tea, and read the newspaper until they came back. It took them about two hours before returning then we left for home again without anymore stopping.

When we reached home the children looked tired and both went for a rest, after waking, they came out, and asked if they can make supper, so I said go ahead sat, and watched the college games on the television. They seemed to have the supper preparation down to a science, with all the ingredients placed on the counter. The children seemed to work well in the kitchen, I did not hear one saying no this goes in before that, ingredient, and everything ran so smoothly. They did not say what dishes were being prepared for supper but then again I did not ask.

The supper made by the children which was a surprise, whatever they made was now completed, and they did not say what it was, but let me taste it, if it missed any ingredients,. After tasting what they made, I had to say it was very good, and never told me what was the name, it was just something they put together all by themselves. I must congratulate you on the marvellous supper you made; now it's my turn the dishes will be washed by me, so you all can relax.

The table got cleared, and started washing the dishes, letting them air dry before putting it away. We sat down watching television, either reading or did something different, later after all activities were over we checked the newspaper to see what was playing at the movies. They were no shows we wanted to see so all stayed home and played a board game, which the children enjoyed a lot. The game went on four two hours before they said that it was time for snack.

The snack break was taken after the game was put away for another time, when they came over we l had different snacks cake, apple pie, and I had tea with it a muffin. We sat and watched the last college football game before the local news came on. The game went into overtime, and must say it was the best college game seen in a while, since the season began, at first it was lopped sided. In the last quarter the team that was losing made a great come back the last couple minutes to tie it, and send it into the overtime of a life time.

The news came on before the interviews began with the two coaches that were good because it was late, after watching the news. We l said good night, checking the doors, making sure it was locked turned in for the night. The next morning we l got dressed and went to church as usual from the time they were young, and which continued every time they came over, sometime they will call and asked to be picked up when they are with their mother.

The church was packed but we were lucky to get, our regular seat, the service got started, and from time to time the late comers strolled in one by one, you can tell that the priest was a bit annoyed by the looks on his face. He did not say so in his sermon, service ended on a positive note, the children saw some of their school friends, and some from different class. They talked for a while and I mingled with a couple of my friends, there to my surprise was the woman, who made a pass at me along with her husband. I made some enquires about him, he was a judge in family court, that to me said it all. The scores of cases he had to preside over no wonder his wife was out there looking for some romance.

I approached them, introduced myself along with the children before we left for home, one of the question Dawn asked was who was that woman. I said she was trying to make a pass at me the other day but told her that I was not interested, now that I know her husband was a judge it felt good. I did not make any advances towards her. We went to our little quaint spot for breakfast since we were out already, and was easier to have someone prepare it, than going home, having to do all the preparation.

After leaving the restaurant we took a slow drive into the country side to see what Mother Nature had for us to see. They were no changes just the sun starting to get hotter by the minute, returning home we settled down. The children started their home work, while I read the Sunday papers, until they were l finished, and we watched the football games on the television. We made friendly bet on teams giving us something to do just for the fun of it, and it turned out before supper time Dawn had won most of the bet.

It was getting close to supper time and it was my turn to make supper, decided some finger food was just right since we were watching the football games, with that in mind made wings, mix veggies, and a salad. They choose their own drinks, supper was done before the next game started, and the table was set out with the food buffet style where everyone helped themselves. I made sure we used paper plates because no one wanted to wash dishes after the games. We ate whenever hungry stepped in, and it was such a good choice. I did not want to leave my seat at anytime because the game was getting heated up with no team dominating each other. It came down to the last couple minutes of the fourth quarter; it was a sad out come for the home team with the visiting team winning the game.

The visiting team won the game in the last minute with a field goal, and felt good about them. I must say it was a good game, after the game we cleared the table, and put away the rest of the food that was left over. The children said they would have it for lunch the next day which was Monday. The children had a good weekend, and were glad to see how happy my outlook was, and hoped when Didi and

Alex came they would get to spend time to know them better; they got their bags packed, ready for school.

The time was around 10:00 pm when the children said good night to me. I stayed up for an hour after they turned in, reminiscing about the week end and must say talking about Didi, and Alex went well without any difficulties, but I would have to wait a little longer to see if they have any change of mind after they meet them both during the Christmas holidays.

I went to bed but kept thinking what the children said to me this weekend. I must say sleeping was not easy since I tossed, and turned before falling asleep. I got up, next morning feeling bit tired, the children were already up, preparing their breakfast, after getting ready prepared mine, which was not much. I usually, stop along the way to get a couple muffins or whatever I needed for snack at the office.

Before leaving the house we made sure everything was turned off so they would be no wasting of electricity, dropped them off to school, and they said good bye and love you. I replied love you too, then I was on my way to work, smiling all along the way to work, at this moment I realized how lucky having the best woman in my life, also my three children, whom I loved very much.

I got into the elevator with some of the workers on my floor, all I looked different this morning which was a good thing. I had to admit to them yes it sure feels good today when the elevator stopped we entered the office and each went to their respectful desk and ate whatever they had in their hands before the work day began, for me it was a very good start of the day. I made a call to Didi, and told her the good news that the children were really looking forward to meet both of them over the Christmas holidays, and I was too.

After talking with Didi my work day started, no phone call for quite some time giving me the opportunity to do some paper work before anyone interrupted me. It was a beautiful day the sun was shining although the weatherman called for rain later, but did not think it would dampen my spirits. The way I was feeling about the relationship between Didi and me, was something I hoped for a long time we were seeing each other, and since finding out t Alex was my son.

After lunch they were some interruptions, one of the managers from the top floor came to see me. He wanted to see if there was any chance the scheduled meeting on Wednesday can be put off for Friday, no problem at all. I had to send an email to the various departments informing them of the change and the meeting has been mover to Friday after lunch about 1:00 pm.

All the departments got the email half hour later, and they forwarded it to me saying that it was ok; everything was set for Friday giving me ample time to get things prepared for the meeting. The work day was coming to a close and was noticeable when the workers started getting they work organized for the next day. It was the sign that said it was almost time to get ready for home. I stayed a little longer to do some more paper work, which needed to get out by tomorrow morning with the first mail delivery.

Just around the time of leaving the phone rang, it was Alex saying hi to me, this is a surprise I said! How did you know to call here? Mom said that you may be staying a bit late to do some work. It is good to hear your voice; mom said we would be spending some time with you in California, yes! Is that ok with you? Yep! As soon as school close I would be expecting you and mom okay. I love you, and looking forward seeing you again, so be good, and I would see you soon, he said goodbye and hang up the phone.

I walked out the door with a bigger smile on my face knowing they would be here within a month. There are things I would have to get ready before they come, shopping for gifts, a Christmas tree, making Christmas holidays a memorable one for both of them. I know for a fact food have to be brought, and every little details have to be looked after without me forgetting anything, meaning I would have to make a shopping list something that I have not made in a long time because shopping for myself does not require one.

When I got home, all the positive thoughts that were on my mind was too much for me to handle. I called Dawn cell phone but got no answer, so I made supper sat, and ate then watched the news just before the news ended, the phone rang it was Dawn calling back to see what the matter was, so the idea that was in my head was relayed to her, and she said that she would go shopping with me to get gifts for Didi and also groceries, and please tell your brother that I will need help to get something for Alex, and that would be his department.

After hanging up the phone, my thoughts were making a grocery list of what was needed in the house for Christmas, remembering all the previous years when I was still married. The amount of groceries that had to be made was very over whelming, at this time with pen in hand the task of making that shopping list began, first was the dairy products, greens, veggies, meats, snacks, breads, cakes, and anything else that was remembered.

It was a good thing I knew someone that caters for people like me who could not make pastries in quantities, placing a call to her put in and order for what was needed. My delivery date was close to the time Didi, and Alex was getting here. The ordering of pastries, were taken care of the next item on the list was the meats. I called the butcher, told him what was needed, and he said no problems it would be ready for you within a week's time, all that I need to look after were the other items on the shopping list.

With all the major items taken care off I relaxed for a while then did the supper dishes, and watched a show on the television, after the show ended I started reading the book I had began, until it was just close to my bedtime. I looked over the list making sure nothing was forgotten, secured the apartment, and went to bed. The phone rang, this time it was Matt, he wanted to know when we were going shopping for Alex gifts, gave him a date told him to pass the message onto his sister. He sound very excited, he was going shopping to get something's he knows his little brother would like.

It has been quite some time since I have seen them so excited about buying gifts, remembering when they were small brought back memories, now that they are older their gifts for Christmas comes in the form on a loaded visa credit card. I put a sum of money so they can spend it on whatever they may need, but most of the time they would buy a few items and save the rest for when they have school or go shopping at the mall with friends.

They also get a few items I think they would need, and this I placed in a Christmas stocking for them so they still get something to open during the Christmas holidays. It was past midnight when my head rest on the pillow, falling asleep was no problem. I got up bright and early in the morning another working day, and the cycle started all over again, and made sure all the morning routines were completed before leaving the house. My only wish was, the week end was here, but it was only the second work day of the week, and it seems as though it was dragging just to spite me.

The drive into work was like any typical morning, the traffic going at a slow pace, and bumper to bumper where all the lights on the boulevard seems to be red when it was my turn to go through the green light. Along the way they were many fender benders, and people just had to slow down, to have a look instead of driving normally, this frustrated quite a number of people and you could hear the horns blowing for a long way off by other drivers that had to get to work.

This was one morning that it was not convenient to stop for anything to eat because it would have made me late, instead I went to the cafeteria down stairs the office building, and get me something to eat. They did not have what I really wanted, but took something that would curb my hunger till lunch time. It was not long before getting to my office when the phone rang; on the other end of the line was that familiar voice which perks me up whenever I hear it. She was calling to inform me of the day they would be leaving Chicago for California. I would make the arrangements for the tickets today, which you should have, no problems receiving it through email.

It was final and the date set, it felt so good knowing both of them would be here sooner than I thought, something that is worth looking forward to, along with my two other children. The day seemed to just drag on slowly by the minute, as if the work day was ten hour instead of eight, but had to make the best of it since they was nothing that could be done no matter if you tried. The more I watched the time it seemed as though the time was not moving any faster since looking at the clock. The next time I looked at the clock the work day was coming to an end which tells me the more you look at the time the longer it takes; this in fact looked like the longest day of any of my work day.

There was no alarm clock letting you know the work day was ending, all you had to do was look at the workers, and you would automatic know, when they start putting things away it was close to the end of the work day. They had a build in timer which all had, and worked in unison with each other. The day ended on a positive note for me, as they all walked out you heard each one telling the other see you tomorrow or have a good evening, and a safe trip home.

The drive home was better than the morning, it was easier to manoeuvre the traffic tie ups that was taking place, and with a faster pace made a stop to get my supper. I did not feel like making supper so take out was the best thing, my favourite today was Chinese food although when you eat their food within an hour you seems to get hungry. It taste so good especially their chicken, and fry rice, after paying for my order it was time to get home to sample my food while watching the early news on the television.

While the television was on I got my plate and dish out the different food, had a drink, sat and watch the news, but because they were only a few items to wash, and put away they remained in the sink until the news was over. I did not wash the dishes until it was close to bed time, after doing the dishes, made sure all was secured, turned the lights off, and proceed to the bathroom before going to the bedroom.

I lay in bed thinking about how the Christmas holidays would go but what it all comes down to is making the best of it. This would be the first Christmas spending time with a woman in the apartment, and glad it was with Didi, Alex Dawn, and Matt, how that would go is something left to be seen. Although we talked about her it is how the children get along with her, and she with them while staying with us in California for the holidays.

I am sure it will go well, but we are l looking forward to that special visit when all can be together just as though we are a happy family. My mind was racing about everything that was needed to do, making those days special and memorable for all to enjoy. There is not much left to do but plan, and hope that it works for the best, without any more thinking, sleep crept up on me, and then my eyes were closed.

The next morning I awoke bright and early, got my morning routine done and left for work earlier than usual, stopped for breakfast before going to the office. At the far end of the restaurant was the judge's wife sitting alone as though she was waiting for someone. I did not look in her direction too much in case she glanced over, and notice me but kept my head down eating. At times look up to see what she was doing, then a gentleman walked in and went straight towards her, who was not her husband I did not know, so who am I to judge what she was up to. After eating proceeded to pay my bill, and as I was leaving she called out to me yoo-hoo, good morning.

I had no other choice but to walk over and said hello, then left for work, it was a wonder that she did not make me out from where she was seated, all the same I was glad that I did not have to sit with her, and hear all her details about her and her husband's problems. The mere fact of seeing her there got me thinking about changing my breakfast habit, seeing that she knew that I was having breakfast they she may visit there a bit more often just to see if I am there alone or with anyone.

At work they were some talk about what was happening at the meeting on Friday, but did not bothered stopping and listening to the conversation. I went straight to my office closed the door and started doing some work, and then all was quiet for a while. They had settled down to do their work for the day no other conversation never came up again for the day. I remembered they were and agenda that had to be circulated to the departmental managers about the meeting on Friday although an email was sent.

That gave me something else to do, and without any hesitation emailed it out to the respectful managers informing them know exactly what we were going to talk about, and the meeting would be about an hour and a half. It would give them time to return to their department and discussed what was said with their staff members. The work day went pretty good and fast without having to look at the clock in the outer office to see the time. It would soon be the start of the dreaded evening drive home routine for all everyone saying to each other drive safe see you tomorrow.

It was normal for me with no one to rush home to, and time on my hands the drive home was pleasant, made a few stops but not for long. I picked up a pizza for supper, since it was only me alone eating it. The moment the key opened the door the phone rang, and rushing to get it the box with the pizza dropped on the floor but did not open, or splattered which was a good thing.

It was Dawn, she wanted to know if she can come by for a visit, I said sure and within a couple of minutes she was there. It was a good thing t I got home early, and bought something with me to eat, she came in, sat and talked for a bit. She also wanted to know what I thought about the university she choose to attend when she graduate this year. She was thinking of staying close to home or going out of state, we talked, and gave her some facts about staying close to home, and also away from home. She thanked me and asked me to take her home after she finishes her homework.

I did not realized how fast the school year went, it was not the lack of not noticing it was a busy year with everything happening to me so fast. I nearly missed the school term, and knowing very soon Dawn, would be attending a university of her choice. Before taking her home we stopped for a treat, talked some more about university living, and what life is on the whole away from home, and what to expect while on campus her first year.

We left after our treat, and while driving home she wanted to know more about Didi, and Alex. We talked about them which eased her mind quite a bit, and had a good feeling about Didi, that she would make a good companion for me, and also a good stepmother, she sound like someone who listens before giving her thoughts on something's. I am proud of her wisdom she has gain over the years while growing up, and knows exactly what she wants to do with her life.

After saying good bye and good night she entered the house, I left, and took a slow drive home admiring the night scene in front of me which I had not seen for a while. I simple did not have the urge to visit that part of town in the night, not long after I got home the phone rang, Dawn, called to make sure I got home okay, something that was instilled into them while growing up as kids. I was glad to know it was still part of they up bringing as they became young adults.

I changed into my pyjamas, and after my night routine went straight to bed until next morning, which came very quickly. They was no rush but was out the door on my way to work, went through the drive through for my breakfast, and proceeded to the office sat, and ate before the morning crowds came in to work. I had time for a quick phone call which was made to Didi just to say hello, and to find out if everything was okay with her.

I said good bye to her when the office staff began getting crowded, it was good hearing her voice which puts me in a good frame of mind during the day. It also helps me get things done in a peaceful way I do not really know why but it does, all I can say is it could be the way how I feel about her, and what she brings into my life at this point of the relationship.

Just think about the way you feel when you are in love for the first time, and you would know what I am talking about. I know everyone who was ever in love has a certain feeling about things, and the way they feel life is going, the relationship with that person feels very real that you cannot wait to be near the person. You find yourself wanting to be ever so close no matter where they are so it is with me.

My work load was not heavy today a few memos and emails that was needed to be sent out. They was a knock on my door, my secretary came in with some papers for my signature. I asked her to leave it on my desk, and would buzz her when they are signed. I must tell you, my secretary is a very beautiful person, from time to time I ask her how she is doing, although single and have been my secretary for almost ten years. She has never made an attempt any kind of relationship with me which I respect.

She stands about five feet eight inches tall weights about one hundred and fifty pounds, and well built, very smart and knows her job that is one of the many reasons she is with me. She is aware and knows all that I went through, and always had a good word for everyone working in the office. They have never had a bad word spoken about her, dresses very professionally, and that is a quality I have not seen in anyone for a long time. She looks like a model, slim built very beautiful, with light brown hair and light tan complexion

Most of you must be thinking with a person right there in your office why not make a pass at her. It is my policy one should not be having any relationship with someone you work with because if and when you do break up then what, the whole office would know. The atmosphere would feel cloudy, and sooner than you think one of you would be asking for a transfer to another department or leave the job, because you cannot stand the person, does that make sense? If it does good if not then you have a thing to learn.

After my secretary left my office, the memos, and the other letters she wanted me to sign were completed, so was the emails and memos that had to be sent out that I had written. It was coming up to lunch time so I buzzed her, told her all the papers she had left was signed, and was ready for sending out. She knocked and entered and asked if she wanted to go out for lunch my treat and agreed to my offer. It was not in any way suggestive, because of the efficiency in her work and appreciated what she did not only for me but the company.

All eyes were on us leaving for lunch, and looked back to see what some of the office staff had on their faces it was simple a smile, nothing was wrong with that. We drove to a small diner which serves wonderful food everyone liked, we talked on the way and she relaxed, and started telling me she once had a crush for me for a while but has wore away. She found some one that has been kind to her, the conversation was mostly about her; at least she was honest to let me know the way she once felt.

When we reached the diner our table was waiting for us, sitting down before the waitress came to take our order we talked some more, as we talked realized she was a home body never went out much until she met the gentleman she is now dating. She told me a little about him, but did not pry or asked any questions more than asked her if she was happy, after ordering she looked at me, and asked how was Didi doing, I said good, she would be spending the Christmas holidays here with me and the children and her son also,. She looked at me and, said good if anyone deserves you it should be her because of the times she kept my secret to herself, which was most appreciated.

While talking I began to know a little more about her, and what part of California she grew up, what surprised me was that the town was not too far from where I lived, before moving to where I am now living. We ate then back to work, entering the building, and office everyone sat and took notice so my explanation was that my secretary was precious to me, and that we went out because she deserves to be treated once in a while by her boss, they all smiled, and acknowledge we do agree with you, and they went back to work. It was a pleasure taking her to lunch after all she was trustworthily in my eyes. It is all that was going to be said on that subject.

The day at the office was coming to an end, and could see from the glass barrier between my office. In the outer office area the workers began gathering up their belongings ready to get out side, and be on their way home. It did not take the offices long to be cleared, and free of anyone except me the last to leave before the office cleaners came to do their job. If there was something that needed to be done I would stay until it was completed.

As I stepped out the office building it had just flashed in my mind thanksgiving was just a couple weeks away, at first not much thought was given about it. I did not make any plans to what or where I was spending the day. On other occasions it would be up in the country with other friends, but this year my decision was to stay close at home. In my thinking of all this special occasion where the tradition was the football games where sport fanatics gathered at home or at a sports bar to drink and watch the games on television. My take on it was to order some takeout pizza, and wings with a few snacks, and stay at home.

All was not lost as yet for that day but the plan was I was not, no going out that day while the game was on, for the next few moments. As I drove home asked myself what was there for supper in the fridge, that can be made quickly, and would not take too much time to prepare. Entering the apartment the first thing I did was opened the fridge, looking to see what was there. At the time eggs looked like a good choice but did not have anything to go with the eggs. I settled for pasta, salad and garlic bread.

The television was turned on while my supper was being cooked, it is amazing the length people would go to get away thanksgiving holidays followed by black Friday a day of pure hell. When the shopping for Christmas presents begins in earnest, this is the worst day of the year to do any shopping; people have no regards for one another. It is like a jungle where everyone fends for themselves. The local news came on showing the crows at the airport there already, the reporter he said this was only the beginning of the thanksgiving rush.

The airline was now in a kind of panic because they had to provide enough planes and schedule more flights in and out of the different airports. The airports in the east was already seeing a surge of people waiting in line to be check in for their flight to take them home to be with relatives or friends that was awaiting their arrival. This happens year after year; while some make other arrangements to drive themselves if it is not long others take the bus or train taking them on their way without the crowds they may encounter at the airport.

The news was over with the replay of the crowd mingling about; some on queue waiting for their tickets to be processed while others was just looking at the board to see if their plane was on time. I turned off the television, and began reading the book that was started sometime back. I read for about an hour then sat, and relaxed before calling Didi, inquiring if she was alright, and also to find out how was her day. We talked for an hour or so then we said good bye, Alex was at his grandparents for the night because his school had a day off the next day.

The week went by fast keeping up with the days seemed impossible one day it is Monday, and before you know it its Friday, meaning tomorrow is the meeting where all managers are supposed to attend. The meeting is vital, with the hopes of talking over some points that came up while talking to staff members a couple weeks back. It was getting close to bed time so making sure all was taken care of, went straight to the bedroom and off to sleep for the busy day that was ahead of me.

I was up bright and early next morning, and left the apartment stopping at my special restaurant for breakfast, this time I went in had a seat, and read the news paper while my breakfast was being prepared. I looked over the papers and in the far corner was the judge's wife; she seems to be a frequent customer here because every time I came in she is there. She was with her husband having breakfast, and a conversation that seems to be going smoothly.

Before leaving the restaurant I gentle wave to them, and headed for my car then off to the office, it was a pleasant morning felt alright with nothing on my mind. It was smooth sailing from here on in most of the staff was at their desks when I walked in a few waved, went straight to my office, and sat took a look at the memos that were in front of me. I signed those that needed my signature, before the secretary came in for them, no sooner it was signed she popped her head in the door, and asked if they were signed, she came in had a seat and to my surprise ask me what I was doing for thanksgiving supper. I told her, and she extended an invitation, she would like me to come over for supper, because she had mentioned me to her mother.

I did felt sort of awkward when she asked, but had to say okay as long as your date is there, oh yes! She said he would be there, and I would like you to meet him, my father mother, and two brothers. She told me the time to be there, took the memos with her then left my office, and went to her station that was in another room, where she did all her work without being disturbed.

After she left my office thought to myself what was I thinking, now that the invitation was accepted the deed was done, so it's no backing out of this one now, at that point? I could have slap myself silly for accepting that invitation, it is just a onetime thing to meet her friends, and family she talked so much about, today of all days the meeting was taking place after launch, and it was a moment to get this of thinking off my mind.

The time seems to take longer during the lunch break, and could not wait for the meeting to commence, where everyone can give an opinion the things that we were going to talk about listed on the agenda. It never occurred to me to ask my secretary to take notes so that we could have it as a reminder what we talked about at the meeting. It was a bit late to ask her now, maybe the next time, why am I all of a sudden trying to get her involved sitting in on the meetings, was there something about her inviting me to her house for thanksgiving that have me feeling kind of guilty about the whole situation.

Enough said about the whole situation it was now time for the meeting, it was being held in the board room, where there are chairs, and table that everyone can sit around taking notes if they wanted to. It was a comfortable room to be in; the meeting started on time and lasted for an hour and a half. Everything on the agenda was talked about some in more detailed than others the most important ones took centre stage and was clarified what a priority was done in the coming year.

The meeting was finished when the time of working came to the end, and we found ourselves mulling around for a while talking about some of the ideas that was discussed. We said our good bye for the weekend which was about to start. It was going to be the start of my shopping for gifts by myself for the three kids, and also to get Didi something I hope she love. I have no idea what it is, but would know when I lay my eyes on it, after leaving work I went to the mall, and started hopping for gifts. The moment I entered this particular store the gift for Didi was staring me straight in the face, there was small grin on my face when I saw the item.

It was late when my shopping was completed, but had to make several trips to the car dropping off the gifts, returning to continue shopping. I was tired by the time I got out of the mall so it was straight home for me to get everything out the car before the children came over tomorrow. The carrying gifts to the house got me a little tired, and had to have a quick rest before continuing; finally when everything was done sat on the couch and relaxed.

The time went and found myself nodding off for a bit, and woke myself up when I started snoring, something that I have not done in a while. The last time I snored was after doing yard work living as a family with Sarah and the kids. The clock on the wall was saying about 11:30 pm, and to tell you the truth, did not think I slept that long. I stayed awake for another hour before going to bed, and slept until 8:30 am which was quite late for me, just after changing my clothes, Dawn called inquiring about the time when they were being picked up.

I gave her a time, and then went straight to make my breakfast, put away the gifts so that they could not be found, grabbing my keys, and locking the door headed straight to get them. We did some more shopping this time they both went shopping for gifts for Didi, Alex, and for each other, although they were on they own it gave me time to get some Christmas cards for them, and also for family and friends. The time moved very slowly, and sat in the food court waiting for the kids, while they shop, and from time to time they would bring the gifts over for me to watch, until they had completed their shopping.

The children shopped till they were hungry, and tired, we had something to eat, after putting the gifts in the car. They were so much people shopping that you would think it was black Friday, but it was a week away, some people could not wait for that special day some said that they just would not be caught dead shopping on black Friday, with all the pushing that the crow had to offer at most of the stores that may have deals that day. It was good to know that all the gifts were bought already, and the only shopping left was the major groceries before Christmas which was a couple weeks away, and I can vision the crow doing the shopping the same time as everybody else.

The thing is some grocery stores I know are open 24/7 so I can do my shopping at night on a weekend without the hassle of the crowd, so with that train of thought the only thing left to do was go home, and un load everything from the car, and have the children start wrapping gifts, with name tags on each so the gifts would not be miss placed. The wrapping of the gifts had taken longer than usual, because we wanted to do a good job with them.

After all the wrapping was completed it was time to relax for the rest of the evening, and later we decided some barbeque ribs, and chicken with mix veggies would be good for supper. I placed a call to the local takeout restaurant, and wait until it came. The moment the food got here we sat in front the television and watched the college football games taking place around the nation on Saturday.

The games went fast each game having half time just about the same time but that did not take away anything from us, between half time. We put away the gifts that were wrapped in the closet so they were out of sight, then we got back to the rest of the games, flipping from one game to another to see if any of our favourite college's were winning their games.

It was not my week to have the kids, but they wanted to shop for gifts today to get it over with, because of the upcoming thanksgiving week they would not have time to help. It was getting late and they were dropped off home so they could do what had to done before Thanksgiving Day arrived. They did ask though what I was doing for that day, and told them t I was invited for supper at one of the office staff home, without revealing who it was to them, all they said was have a good time.

Returning home after dropping them off I put away the rest of the left over's for the next day, then sat and watched the rest of the football games. It was not bedtime as yet but sleep started to creep in so of to bed I went without giving it any thought, next morning as usual it was time for church. I went for the 8:30 am mass, and then had breakfast at my favourite restaurant, before returning home, where I sat, and read the newspaper before the Sunday pregame football shows before the actual football games started for the day. It was a good thing that they were left over food, and was glad I did not have to prepare anything to eat just warm thing up sit, eat and enjoy the games.

The weekend ended too quickly I was just starting to relaxed, thinking that the next day is the start of a new working week, but at the same time it is a short work week due to thanks giving day falling on a Thursday. Many of the workers would be thinking of leaving early getting a head start to see family on Tuesday the latest day being Wednesday for that whole weekend. They would be returning early Sunday hopefully, it was now the first day of the short work week, and was looking forward having supper with my secretary, her family, and her new boyfriend. I would see what he looks like, and also see if he is worthy of her friendship, not to say I would be jealous in anyway.

It was not a very quiet day at the office everyone was talking about where, and who they were visiting this thanksgiving weekend. It seems that those who were going away did not care much about leaving on any trip that was far away. It was not surprising the majority of the workers were driving to their destination which was about two or three hours from their homes, as for me I was glad my trip was not out of town. The time was slowly creeping up to lunch; I made a call to Didi, and asked how she was doing, and if she and Ales were going over to her parent's house for thanksgiving, which was a clear yes. I asked how Alex was doing, she said fine, but kept telling his friends he was going to California for the Christmas holidays.

After talking to her I had the rest of the left over's for lunch what little was left from Sunday. I got caught up with all the paper work that needed my signature, so my day could be free to accept any staff members that wanted to talk. It was unbelievable no one ever came in which was good in a sense leaving me with my thoughts about why did I accept that invitation for thanksgiving. I put that thinking aside called Didi again, and told her about the invitation that I got from my secretary, and she said that it was fine with her me going to dinner, because she trust me knowing nothing would happen.

The day was over, this time tomorrow every one that was going away would want to leave as early as possible which would be fine either way. Driving home the restaurant was better to have supper than me preparing it at this time. I did not know what was at home I wanted to eat; at the restaurant there are choices to choose from. The waitress brought the menu, and without any thought ordered a smoothie to go along with my supper, sitting while my supper was being prepared ahead of my direction was the judges wife, it so happened she saw me walked over, and asked if she could join me, and I said yes but have to leave right after eating. She understood alright, they were only small talk nothing of substance but I could tell she was still trying to make another pass at me but knew better.

After supper I went home, and thought about thanksgiving supper, and although the day was getting closer the excitement began to build, asking myself what it was going to be like, was it going to be alright with the whole situation. The day was not too far off as it got closer I was reminded again of the time supper was going to be served, and they would expect me to be there fifteen minutes early, and not the time they set for supper.

All the chips was falling into place and my comfort zone was now in play do I make myself uncomfortable in their presence or feel a bit jittery, that is something that would have to be played out at the time of my arrival. The day was finally here, and was looking forward not only for supper but to meet all her family and friend that she spoke about these past couple weeks when we chatted, most of all I wanted to hear how she would introduce me to her parents, and family, also her new found male friend that she talked about.

I left home early giving myself sufficient time to get there, driving the speed limit, sometime slower and got there without any difficulties, right on time. I pulled into the drive way, the house sat quite a distance from the road and was very private with trees in front the house, pulling up to the house the door opened, my secretary stood in the doorway waiting for me at the door. We walked inside, and were introduced to her family along with her male friend; they made me felt welcome as though we had known each other for quite a long time.

I felt very comfortable talking to them and discussed the football games that were going to be played on television. We were called for supper, the meal was great the usual thanksgiving dinner most families sit down to, but this one had a twist to it. I had to say the prayer before supper, it was something they do when they invite any guest, and the guest has to say the prayer. I do not know what religion they were, and did not asked but sat with the family to a great thanksgiving meal.

After the meal and the table cleared the ladies went into the kitchen putting away any left over's while the men headed for the basement to watch the football game. After the ladies completed the task they were doing they joined us, and we sat and watched the game discussing the other team strategy when they get the ball. The evening was well spent as the time passed on found me drawn to the family in a way not because I was asked to come for dinner but felt connected to them in some sort of way, with their mannerisms which our family also exhibited.

I did not want to over stay my welcome, after the second game thanked them for inviting me for supper, that I had a great time knowing them. I can see where your daughter get her strength and looks from with that a little chuckle broke out, my secretary walked me to the door after saying good-bye to everyone. After exiting the door turned to her and said you have a great man in your life she thanked me very much for that observation, and gave me a peck on the cheek, said see you at work next Monday.

On my way home it really felt good knowing what I thought was going to be uncomfortable turned out to be a great evening with a family I hardly knew. My guess was their daughter had talked so highly about me for a long time now, and that they have met me it was considered a pleasure. I must say it came as a surprise to me when they all called me by my first name. It was nice knowing the evening turned out to be a great one, pulling into my drive way the lights to my apartment was on, but did not know if by chanced it was left on when leaving earlier.

The only thing I could think of was one of the children was there, because both have keys so they can come over anytime they chose. It is something I wanted, giving them the privilege to do so whenever they want. I unlocked the door and walked in but no one was there. It must have been me that left a light on nothing was moved or looked unfamiliar in any way. I sat down relaxed for a bit then the phone rang it was my secretary calling to see if I got home safe and to thank me again for coming.

It felt a bit awkward, she called to talk, and she had never done this before, although she has my number just in case she needed me to sign memos or letters that were related to work. She said good night and hung up, a little puzzling to me at first but it made sense it was something that must have been taught by her parents calling to find out if their guest got home safe. It is something we all do from time to time and was good to know that the family was thinking that way, looking out for their guest.

I did not give it another thought, made a call to Didi, but was not at home. I called over to her parents home, wished then a Happy Thanksgiving day, spoke to Didi, then Alex came on to speak with me for a while, after talking gave the phone back to his mother said our good-bye, and promised to call her over the weekend before the end of the weekend.

The weekend came fast and as promised called Didi, spoke to her after speaking sat and watched the football games, and also watched the local news to see what was happening around the city. I cleaned the dishes in the sink and went to bed so I can face another day at work. I arose the sound of my alarm, and did my morning routine had breakfast and was on my way to work, without stopping for carry out from the restaurant.

The parking lot at the office was almost empty, most of the employee's was out of town for their thanksgiving dinner with family, and so it was nearly every year. The day after the first working day of thanksgiving the work force was always up to full staffing. It is amazing what little staff is on hand and how quiet the office is very rare that happens, giving staff time to get caught up with work they left before leaving for thanksgiving holidays.

It was a slow day for me but had some work to catch up on, and was about to do so when my secretary knocked on the door, came in with some other papers that needed signing. We talked about the dinner for a while, and left after the papers were signed, much to my thinking she did not asked me anything about her male friend. Although I told her, she was very lucky to have him in her life; any regrets on my part none whatsoever. I did not see any attraction to her in anyway.

The month was coming to an end in a couple days, my thoughts would was getting everything ready for Didi, and Alex visit, which would be soon and before I know it that day would be here, slowly creeping up without giving me any notice. The week went by so rapidly with all the staff back in full force it was good to see them busy at what they liked, and the time was coming up for their bonus. I had to make arrangements with the accounting department to start getting it ready, because they looked forward having it the second week of December.

Everything was now in place when the second week came around each person got their bonus, and was surprised at what they received reflecting the company's progress along with the profits it made over the course of the year. It was a delight seeing their faces lots of smiles and talking among themselves what they were going to do with their bonus they had received.

In another week or so the office would be closing for Christmas, and I am looking forward to it Didi and Alex would be here spending their holidays with the children and me. They would get to meet their little brother and he their other siblings which they are looking forward to with great expectations. I cannot wait to see both of them again it seems as though a whole year has passed since last seeing them.

All my thoughts was on them and is hoping that everything goes well with their travels, from here on in it would be nail biting time until we actually see each other in person. There are a few more things that needs getting it would have to be done before Christmas, the most important shopping has been taken care of for some time now, what was needed at this point were the vegetables and some groceries that would last us during the holidays.

My daughter and son are expected to give me a hand on the day I am ready which could be within a week or a couple days before they arrive. The shopping and everything that is needed would be in the house ready for when they show up. The days are certainly closing fast and it would be Christmas soon. I did not call Didi for another two days because I did not want her to know how anxious it made me knowing she would be here.

In the days that was ahead of us Dawn called wanting to know what day we were going shopping, and she told me whenever it was convenient the day was set aside baring no problems. The day finally arrived and we went shopping, and had a good time together, had supper then home to unload the groceries. The hard part was finding place for all that we had bought it seemed as though we had bought too much because we had no place to it all.

We had run out of space, went over to the hardware store purchased a shelving unit we think would hold the remainder of the groceries.

It was a good thing the unit we bought had five shelves, and they were enough space to hold everything and some left over room that could be used if we purchased anymore items. It was a good day shopping all the groceries are in place, and was time to relax for a while before taking them home, so that they can do their home work before school closed for the Christmas holidays.

The children were dropped off after shopping; helping me put away the groceries, and supper. I returned home after watched the late night news, before going to bed. The next morning it did not feel like a Saturday, after having breakfast read the newspaper and relaxed, thinking what is there to do now that everything has been completed for the arrival of Didi, and Alex in the next coming weeks, which I was definitely looking forward to without a doubt.

For most of the morning after reading I began tidying up making it look clean as possible for them arrival, and hardly any rushing to do. I told myself with her in my life t there is no other person that matters, but had to convince myself of that. I made a call to Didi after all my work was done just to say hello, when the phone rang they were no answer after leaving a message hung up.

I stayed inside since the impulse was not there to venture outside, and watched a few shows on the television, before the college football games started. It looked as though the time was hovering, and not moving, and time stood still for a long time then suddenly the next time I looked at the clock it was 4:30 pm. The phone rang, approximately three times before answering sure enough it was Didi calling back to talk, it was a brief conversation before hanging up.

The football games were on different channels but watched the ones that were rivals, and switched channels to see how the games were doing during halftime. I made a couple sandwiches and put a couple snacks in front of me along with a drink, and continued watching the games. I did not move from the couch except using the washroom to empty my tank when they were turnovers during the games, which was very seldom on one team frequently on the other team.

In between the games I thought what it would be like having both Didi, and Alex here for the holidays, and can say this it should have been done a long time ago knowing how we felt about each other, after my divorce. I can only wait and see what the outcome would be l when they both come and the interaction that takes place between four of them being together for the first time now that they knew a little about each other. My hopes are that all goes well when they are here for the holidays, making it the most memorable one in a long time for me.

Most of the football games were almost over it was fourth quarter and less than five minutes left. I watched the most interesting one that were tied and coming down to the wire to see which one of the teams would have the best chance of winning the game between the rivalry. I was rooting for the underdog my hopes were with them having the ball they would march down the field and make a field goal to win the game. At this point it did not look good for them, with a turn over, and a couple minutes to go the other team tried a long field goal and won the game by three points.

With the games just about over it was time to tidy up the kitchen, which I did, and left the apartment for a walk around the block. I returned in time to hear the phone ringing, it was Dawn, requesting that they be picked up for church in the morning she hung up after saying good night to each other. The morning came pretty fast with the sun shining very bright this time of the year got dressed, after the morning ritual picked them up for the 8:30 am mass which we always attend, ever since they were small.

After mass ended we went for breakfast at our favourite restaurant, they both ordered a big breakfast, my guess, they were hungry. We talked about anything they wanted to talked about, Matt wanted to know the day Didi, and Alex was coming so he can come with me to the airport, Dawn decided on that day, she would stay at the apartment to welcome them home. Our breakfast order took around twenty minutes before it was brought to us, giving us ample time to talk to each other.

During the time we were eating not a word was spoken, we were concentrating mostly on our food than anything that was on our mind. After our breakfast our conversation started where we had left off Dawn, and Matt wanted to take Alex to the movies when he arrives which was good. It would give them time to actually get to know each other better and to observe his reaction with them.

It is not that often you see two families coming together and the other wanting to get acquainted with the other. It is usually a wait and see attitude and the interaction with the elder children. They wanting to take that initial step to meet their little brother for me, can be a good thing, with that understanding both had agreed after being told about their brother Alex.

The weeks flew by as the hours ticked on; it was very close for the arrival of Didi, and Alex first visit to California. If all goes according to plans they would be here in a couple days which we are anxiously waiting. I could not help thinking what they would like to do when they arrive, would it be straight home or have something to eat, since this would be a long flight my gut instant would be home and relax.

The phone rang at my home office, it was Didi calling to tell me everything was in order, and the flight would be leaving on time if there were no issues. I kept my fingers cross most of the day after we hung up, and getting back to what I was doing had a big smile on my face from time to time. It was definitely a happy moment in my life thinking the woman in my life would be arriving very soon to spend Christmas holidays with me and my children.

The day for their arrival came very fast as though it was willed and anxious as I was it felt good. The plane left on time and would be landing in about four to five hours if the weather cooperates, no storms were predicted. It is known that winter conditions could be very unpredictable at anytime so I prayed it would be a pleasant trip with no unforeseen circumstances would taking that would cancel their arrival.

It looked like a long wait, me being anxious it just goes to show how waiting on anything can be not as though they would be a problem with the weather from here but one cannot tell what may happen on any given moment. It may look fine one minute then bad weather can step in on the drop of a dime. My fear was although the plane would be leaving on time the weather can change in Chicago without warning at times.

I kept checking the airline website to see if the plane left on time and it had so my fear of it not leaving was alleviated at that point. I was looking forward driving to the airport to pickup get Didi, and Alex when the time came. In the mean time they were other things needing to be taken care of, so with time on my hand tried to accomplished it before it was time for me to get the children to bring them over here, and have Matt accompanied me to the airport to pick up his little brother, and Did on their arrival.

The time seemed as though it had not moved at all, but it was my thinking. It was only a mind game being played on me, and it was a waiting game that had to be played out. I began counting down the minutes the plane would be arriving, and the time that was needed to leave for the airport to greet them after clearing their luggage on their arrival. The time came for us to leave, my heart began to race at a fast pace, being anxious to see them again. I caught myself driving a little too fast, just to be there on time.

As we got into the airport waiting area it was announced the plane would be arriving on time. We looked for a seat and waited for the plane to touch down. The passengers disembarked and entered the exit door to the area where everyone else was waiting for their family, or friends. In front of me they both stood looking around to see if they had seen any familiar face they knew, and at that point walked towards them, gave Didi a hug, and Alex a hand shake welcoming then to California.

I introduced Didi, and Alex to Matt they both looked at each other for a while before they started chatting, Matt took the time to know Alex while we were driving to the apartment. Alex really warmed up to Matt, as though he knew him for a long time it was good to see them started talking. A lot of questions were asked and answered between them. It was not too far in the distance I explained to Didi, and Alex we should be home shortly where Dawn was waiting to greet them, and they could not wait to meet her.

As I turned into the drive way Dawn was outside as though she had timed us on our arrival. She was waving to Alex as we pulled in and park the car, was introduced to both and was no surprise they both hit it off well. They l started talking wanting to know how their flight was. It was amazing how well they all got along after seeing one another for the first time. It seemed they were both accepted, and that was nice, as though we were a family for a long time but Didi, and Alex was away for a while and now that they are here they fit in perfectly with us, that is. It is exactly what I had hoped for, and it was good to see it working that way.

At this time they is not much to say more than to give a toast welcoming them here, and hope their stay with us would be a memorable one. We had to think about supper and what we were going to have they were two choices I could prepare supper or order out, but all were in agreement to have me prepare supper.

We sat around the table talking, eating, and making plans for what we were going to do in the coming days. The children invited Alex to see a movie of his choice that was only one day planning Didi and I said that we would stay home the day they planned to go out. It would give us some time to talk about what we were going to do while she was here, and if she had any plans to visit places of interest.

The time spend talking went fast that we paid little if any attention to it after eating we cleaned up the dishes and kitchen then settled on the couch while the children continued talking. It was interesting to see them getting along as though they knew each other for a long time. It was also good to see them laughing and playing games with each other. The amazing side of it was the kindness they showed to Alex, and Didi as though they were here on several occasions before and knew them for quite a while but today was the first time meeting.

My relationship with Didi, and Alex meant a lot to me and both children saw that it was, and was glad t it was Didi, and not any other person from around here. It would have made things very awkward for their mother and in a sense I am glad it was too. The holiday season is not into full swing as yet, and very soon the carolling will began and the voices of happy people will be greeting each other as they pass, saying season greetings, or merry Christmas.

One way or another it was plain to see the city, and nearby neighbourhood all lit up bringing in the season of great joy. The lights on the boulevard were multicoloured, which enhanced the city as it transfer from dull the last couple day to that of a peaceful surroundings. The people appreciated the brightness and colours of the light as it shone brilliant in the night, the children wanted to continue talking and they wanted to sleep in the living room. We brought up the air mattresses we camp with everyone pitching in and when it was completed Didi and I said good night to them.

One thing that was said before retiring for the night was they could not talk until the wee hours of the morning although l schools were closed. My office was closed the same period as the schools and this was good for the parents that had shopping to do before the Christmas rush starts, in the next couple days.

The lights in the living room were turned off and the children voices could be heard, with lots of giggling and talking, what they were talking about only they knew. Didi and I laid in bed talking e about thing that would affect us if we decide to get married, she had thought about that also, and came to a decision if and when we do get married she would like a transfer to another office if possible., or even work in the same area with another company if they was a job opening. I would call around and see if they are any opening, in fact some people I knew owed me a favour.

We laid in bed she on my chest, and my arms around her, with nothing much to do we caress and kissed each other from time to time, at one point the place got hotter as though we wanted to have sex. We thought of the children in the living room as the saying goes when the time is right. We gave it our best shot having sex without the children knowing what was going on with. It was something missed by both that passion, and ecstasy came alive with all that we had to give each other the waiting was well worth it.

We fell asleep after cleaning ourselves up we did not leave the bedroom which would have given the children some indication what went on in the bedroom. It was late when we all got up the next morning, everyone that slept in the living room looked tired, when asked the time they went to bed they said in unison around 2:00 am, no wonder they looked tired. We gave them a little time to get some more sleep into their system.

The children slept until 9:00 am then they put away the air mattresses, cleaned up then they were ready for breakfast. They wanted something simple like cereal and toast and orange juice, Didi, and I had the morning special ham, eggs, homemade fries and toast along with a cup of tea. After eating the children said they were going out, off they went all three, they took the bus leaving us home to talk and do whatever we wanted to do or go some place we decide on.

Didi decided she wanted to visit the mall, after cleaning up the kitchen and changing clothes we drove to the mall which was about twenty minutes. It took much longer today than usual as though everybody was out shopping. It was hard getting a parking space. When we arrived and had to wait for at least ten minutes to get a spot. We entered the mall after parking and in the corridor were hordes of people shopping for Christmas it was impossible at times to get into some stores so we pass them for another one.

We had just finished shopping at the fourth store when I got a tap on my shoulder, turning around were my secretary (Delores) and her boy friend Nicklaus. I introduce Didi to them, and the two women began talking and decide to hand us men the bags to hold. They were empty seats at the food court so we let the women go shopping r until they were ready to call it a day shopping. We sat down had a tea and pastries, and talked about what was happening for the holidays.

The women returned from shopping after three hours both looked exhausted, but it was a good for Didi and Delores to get acquainted since she knew the voice and was now putting a face to it. Delores knew a lot more of Didi than Didi knew of her the only things Didi knew of her is what I mentioned. They both sat, had a cool drink and something to snack on, we talked for a while then Didi whisper something to me and I said ok. Didi extended an invitation that both of them can join us after Christmas for supper and a drink on Boxing Day.

It was good seeing them getting along together, and I am sure they would keep in touch when she goes back to Chicago. I would have to watch everything I do from here on in, everyone was finished with their snacks, and it was time to go we said our good bye and wish them both a happy holiday, out to the parking lot. The cell phone rang, Dawn wanted to know where we were, after our conversation I told Didi we had to pick them up not too far from here, but the road was so jammed with traffic that it took a while getting them.

It was approaching close to supper time, and I did not want to rush back to prepare supper after getting the children we went to one of our favourite restaurant, this was Didi's, and Alex's first time eating out. It was good knowing after we were seated and Didi looked at the menu nod to me, she liked what was on the menu. The waitress came over took our orders and welcome Didi, and Alex to California, our orders were given to the chef's, and did not take long before we started eating.

The conversation was a good one between the children, and Didi I listened to what they were saying to each other now and again said something but it was mostly between the children, and Didi. They was not much to say more than ask if everyone was enjoying their supper, all saying yes one after the other and asked about desert. I gave in to their demands knowing they had the best desert in the neighbourhood especially the ice cream and apple-pie.

The supper and desert were delicious, and enjoyed by all not much was left to do the bill was paid and we left for home. We got home safe and sound and everything taken out of the car, reclined to the couch and chairs to relax since they were nothing left to do. We waited for the news to come and see the daily happenings taking place around the city for the holiday season. The day was well spent by all and watched the news after it was finished the children watched a show one of their favourite that was on television.

Didi and I watched the show with them until it was over then went into the room to talk and the laughter coming out from the living room was never heard so loud before. It was good hearing and seeing them having so much fun together that they did not want it to stop. Dawn, and Matt had to go home for the night but would be back in the morning when they were ready to leave, we went to the car, so they could be driven home. They did not lived too far from me that was good it was a bit late and I did not want them catching the bus that time of the night.

Returning home Alex said he was tired and was going to bed since he went to bed late last night the latest that he had ever stayed awake. He hugged us both and was off to bed, when we looked in on him he was fast asleep, now it was our turn but we were not that sleepy. We talked until sleep began to overcome us turned off the lights and went to bed. Alex was sleeping in the far bedroom, we started to get naked and get down to some serious sex which we could not have done last night.

That passion and ecstasy once shared came back and started to get on with our love making. The pure joy of it all was such a rush the movement of the up and down action sent the joy and pleasure straight to her and with a low sound had an orgasm little while after I had that pleasure of ejaculating. It was a sure sign of what we meant to each other the fact we can came together and share our feelings was good. We continued for a while again, after having another passionate feeling with love making we cleaned up then went to bed in each other arms.

We awoke early the next morning, looked in the room Alex was still sound asleep. We made our way to the kitchen sat at the table and sip our tea till he got up. I went for the papers and began reading, after sitting down the phone rang it was Matt, he said they would be coming over around noon which was fine for us.

Alex awoke at 10:00am and said that he was very hungry, and wanted a big breakfast consisting of eggs, home fries, toast, and bacon with a cup of tea. We both had the same, since he wanted all that it was easier making it for all, He did his morning routine changed in to clean clothes, and came out for breakfast said good morning, sat down at the table and started eating. He did not utter a word until he was completely finished eating, then asked if his sister and brother was coming at what time. We told him said cool! Then he relaxed until they arrived.

Any plans for today I asked? I do not have a clue what is in store for today he replied, Ok! Then I continued eating. The dishes were cleaned up and kitchen tidied before the children came over, they did not have anything planned for today but wanted to take a drive to our favourite hiking trail. The whole gang decided that it was a go so off we went. The three children walked together on the trail and Didi, and I walked behind keeping an eye on them as they walked, talking to each other stopping to enjoy the site along the way.

Didi and Alex had never gone walking on any trails in Chicago, because they were far away from where they lived. The opportunity came up they said yes, it was good to see them enjoying the walk. When we reached our favourite spot, we sat for a while and took in more of the scenery and site of the valley below far away from us. It was breathe taking with the cars going by on the freeway with their lights on.

The children went exploring nearby where they could be seen and Didi and I talked about whatever came to our minds, and how we felt about each other and what was the next step from here. My surprise was she asked what I had in mind, I asked her if she would marry me, the answer that was received was not the one expected it was yes. We did not say anything to the children, it was not the right time to tell them, so we decide to tell them on Christmas day sometime when we are gathered for supper.

After our talk we called the children, because it was time to go it was pass lunch time and I am sure hunger was about to step in soon. We walked holding hands down the trail to the car the children noticed, but said nothing about it. My guess was they were expecting to see us holding hands some time during their stay here by us holding hands told them that we were serious about each other, and wanted them both in my life as a family.

We drove for a while, came to our quaint mom and pops restaurant we normally ate at when we did hike, not that we had to eat there, because the food was that great. It was not busy today which was a good thing for us, on entering we were greeted by the owner who wished us happy holidays.

We returned the favour, and then were seated, with menus in hand; we looked it over and waited to see what the rest were going to order. My order was always the same this time instead of fries I had a baked potato, the rest of the gang order hamburgers with sweet potato fries, and shakes. The food was good everything you put into your mouth seemed to just melt, and no chewing required, that is how good the food was and tasted out of this world.

We took the time to savor every bite that was in our mouth, and not long after the children had eaten they asked for another burger, because they were still hungry. I did feel like the children but did not reordered, Didi did but not a burger she tried the hot dog they made especially for the Christmas season. After we were filled and paid for the food the children went to have a look at the fish the owner stocked in the back yard pond. They went; we followed right behind walking the way lovers do when they are in love with each other. The children did not asked any questions at all but just enjoyed us holding hands, for some reason or the other Dawn suspected something but did not ask. It was left at that, with no questions asked and no answer given because they were none to give.

It took us twenty minutes to drive home taking a different route avoiding the traffic on the road we normally take, it was a slower drive compared to the normal route because of the holiday rush. I thought it was better to go the route that was taken. We reached our final destination home, and all got out of the car headed straight for the door everyone making a pit stop, before sitting to watch the news on the television. The news was showing the crowds at the malls, and the people that were frustrated because they could not find what they had seen a couple weeks before. It was all due to the mad Christmas rush along with the sales that were going on, leaving people spell bound. I am so glad we shopped a long time ago, so that we could avoid the rush. We knew it was going to happened, on a day like this seeing that in a couple of day it would be Christmas day, and they would be the last minute shoppers trying to find items they had put off buying they had seen. It is always the last minute shoppers I felt sorry for some of them would surely be disappointed.

The children wanted to watch a movie after the news, which was fine with Didi, and myself it was a movie they had not seen before, Dawn being the eldest of the three, made enough popcorn to munch while the show was on. They sat on the floor each with their own bowl of popcorn, and watched the show while eating their fill of popcorn. It was thrilling to see them each with their own bowls and when they had finished eating they paused the movie, went for a drink each having a different kind, resuming where they had left off.

It was a three and a half movie it overt late, and they wanted to repeat the same sleeping arrangements they had when Alex came. They got the air mattresses made them up and laid down while Didi, and myself sat on the couch, listening to them talk about their day, and what they were going to do with Alex. Dawn and Matt had arranged to meet some friends at the local eatery where they hang out and wanted Alex to meet some of their friends that was settled and was ok for them to take him along.

Since we had a busy day Didi and I turned in for the night, but the three children wanted to talk some more about the time they were going to leave in the morning. Then suddenly they were quietness, and knew they had fallen asleep, with no spoken words, only silence. It was time for us to do the same, although Didi was next to me it felt as though she was far away, my guess was t she was thinking about her parents because this was the first time she and Alex were not spending Christmas with them.

The next words to her was you should call your parents in the morning before Alex goes out so he can wish them a merry Christmas, and you can give then the good news. We said good night to each other with a kiss, and lying in each other arms fell asleep. In the morning e we could hear voices coming from the living room and the clinking of pots, pan, and dishes; to our surprise when we walked out into the kitchen breakfast was being made by all three children as a well oiled unit. The fact was they were doing this as though they had done this together knowing Dawn she took charged of the whole thing. It was an experience Alex would never forget for some time to come.

Didi called her parents after we had finish breakfast, before the children left to meet their friend, both wish them season greetings, Alex said good bye to his grandparent and they were out the door, at this point Didi had not tell her parent anything. She talked to her mother where she went, who she met, and then she said to her mother! I have some good news to tell you Drew has asked me to marry him, and my answer was yes! Well congratulations to you both. We have not told the children, but we are going to wait till Christmas day, with a little joyful tear trickling down her cheek said goodbye love you mom, and will talk to you soon, then hanged up the phone.

The children were now out of the house, and we sat talking something magical came over us at that moment. We knew t it was the time to have our magical moment together, we went into the bedroom, and let the magic of having sex come to us. It was the most beautiful experience we ever had with all the passion, ecstasy, and adrenaline flowing came that burst of energy followed by a great orgasm moment. We took a few minutes to recuperate, then we back having sex which we both enjoyed during the late summer months.

The mere fact is we had not seen each other for a while brought out the tiger, and tigress in us and without any hesitation began the sexual ritual over again until that special moment. We climaxed together to the beautiful sound of oooooh! We lay on our backs in each other arms before taking a shower. We got dressed and waited for the three children to return. It was a short time after getting dressed the phone rang; Dawn was on the other end, telling me they would be home within two hours.

That was fine, we had not planned to go anywhere until you all came home, she said good-bye, and we sat on the couch holding hands. We were thinking how to tell the children what was our decision, it made sense to tell the children after we had supper on Christmas evening. It was a happy moment in her life, and with a smile on her face buried her head on my neck, if that is not happiness then what was it?

I cannot imagine what the children are going to say when we tell them, but I will bet there would say congratulation to both of us welcoming Didi, and Alex as part of the family. There will be no hesitation on their part; seeing the three of them attached to each other was no surprise at all that kind of relationship can only happen when there is love within both parties.

They were the gangling of keys, the door was unlocked and they came in one behind each other, sat down, and Alex began talking about the friends he met while hanging out with his sister and brother. He had a wonderful time with them they were starting to get even closer to each other as the days went, and much to my surprise Dawn said to me, when he goes home she would miss him. She had gotten closer to him in a special way not as a big sister but one she cared about, Matt on the other hand said it in a similar way, which tells me that they love each other very dearly.

The boys went into the bedroom to watch television, and Didi went in my room to have a nap until supper time. Dawn, and I remained in the living room chatting, while we were chatting I asked her a question, what do you think about Didi? Her answer was dad you both looked happy with each other, and I do like her a lot, she is warm and beautiful in a lot of ways. I think you two deserved each other, wow! That was good to hear just then the boys came out to see what we were doing.

All of us started making plans for supper, and what we were going to have, they all said chicken, vegetables, rice with baked beans and a salad, ok that is settled. They were willing to do a part Matt did the vegetables Dawn the salad, and Alex set the plates and utensils on the table while I got the chicken started. It was going to be a surprise chicken dish that I never made for quite a long time, and everyone was anxiously waiting to see the outcome of it, while it was being baked the children sat and watched television until supper was ready.

The smell of the chicken woke Didi up and came out to see what was happening, she could not believed the children had done all the food preparation, and Alex setting the table. The chicken was done on time and sat down for supper at 6:00 pm said prayers before meals, and began digging in. The chicken was tender that the meat was dropping off the bones all looked and tasted delicious, and thanked them for pitching in and doing their part. We had a good conversation at the table and when we were finished eating, and clearing the dishes we had desert to end our supper.

At this time everyone was full and satisfied with no one hurrying to leave the table. We continued the conversation about any topic that came up. The day was coming to an end soon Dawn and Matt would have to leave because they usually spent Christmas Eve, and Christmas morning at home, and spend Christmas Eve and Boxing Day with me. It was good now that Alex and Didi was here it would make that day much happier and pleasant.

It was time to take the children home, Dawn asked if it was ok for Alex to come over to see where they lived before I can answer he said can I! I said that is ok. The children got into the car Didi, said that she would stay home till I returned. The road was very clear and the traffic was stop and go, most of the people working at the malls were on their way home to spend a quiet evening with family because of the hectic day they may have had at the stores.

I returned home faster than I went, then ask him what he thought about his sister and brother. It turned out that he like them so much he was going to miss them when it was time for him to leave. That is telling me t he had really gotten close to them in such a short time and to me that is bonding without any doubt knew what a special person he was and they had for him in return.

The circumstances could have been worse, it turned out better than was expected with the love that was shown by Dawn and Matt to Didi and, Alex. It gave me a sense that all was going to be well with us as a family if we got married. We had so much to do and say the next day, the baking of the food and whatever we needed to get done, we turned in for a good night sleep knowing come tomorrow would be a very hectic day.

We said good night Alex did the same said that he love us both, then went off to his room. I waited for about an hour when I thought he was sleeping, went to the basement and started bringing up the gifts, placing them under the tree for the next day. I made sure that the gifts would be there when everyone awoke, and fell asleep the minute my head touched the pillow with Didi laying beside me, we cuddled while we both slept.

The next morning they were a knock at the door, and a voice said wake up sleepy head its Christmas day, ho ho ho! We came out and there he was looking for his gifts Santa had brought him. I said you can open a couple and leave some for when Dawn and Matt came later this evening for supper. It was a good two hours before making breakfast consisting of pancakes, sausages, and eggs we sat, ate and talked for a while before clearing the table and Alex said thanks to his mother and me for his gifts, he had to wait until the other two children came over to thank them also.

The breakfast dishes were washed and put away, while Alex played with the gifts he received, Didi and I began the Christmas dinner preparation before the children got here. It was good to see her doing some house work alongside me; it gave me such a wonderful feeling knowing that the kitchen could hold the two of us comfortable. She started making the pastries, while I prepared the main course, consisting of a ham, veggies, mash potatoes, Cole slaw, salad, sweet potatoes, and a slew of other good stuff to many to mention.

It took both of us about four hours to prepare the stuff now it was time to start baking the ham along with the other items that needed baking. The first to go into the oven was the pastries just to get it out of the way before the children got here. She made some dinner rolls and a couple apple pies one was for today dinner, and the other for tomorrow. She invited Delores and Nick over for a drink on Boxing Day, so we made sure there were enough not only for today but for a couple days into the New Years.

Soon it would be time for Dawn, and Matt to arrive Alex was anxiously awaiting their arrival, because he kept looking through the window to see if they had arrived. The last time he looked and walked away they showed up when he heard the keys opening the door he ran to it. He gave them a big hug and wished them both a Merry Christmas. It goes without saying that he really missed them quite a bit since getting attached to them; they exchanged gifts and had a laugh or two while doing it.

While all this was taking place the foods was being placed in separate dishes and into different bowls that was suited for the occasion. It was a grand feast for today, and from where I am standing had more than enough for left overs that we did not need to cook for a couple days. It was mentioned by Dawn whether or not we were going to do something for New Years Eve, if so what were the plans, so we said let's talk about it over supper, which was fine with her

It looks as though she had gotten the bug for going place, and was good she wanted to make Alex feel at home, while he was here spend Christmas with them. Everyone helped set the table or put the food on the table sitting down for supper, we both had an announcement to make to the children. We had talked about getting married, and asked Didi and she said yes, they both congratulate us and wish us well, that the two of us deserved each other because they saw how happy we were together.

After telling the children I pulled the ring out from my pocket and doing the traditional thing knelt on one knee and pop the question, without any hesitation she said yes! The tears flowed from her eyes for sheer joy on this joyous day of the Christmas season. This is one day she would not forget nor the children because they were part of the joyous occasion and a special one not only for me, but for all at hand. She showed some nervousness as we began eating her hands were shaking and excused herself and went into the bathroom to have a quiet time, washed her face, and returned to the table, and began eating as though nothing happened.

All the while she kept looking at her ring that was now placed on her finger; she was so happy and kept looking at the children and myself acknowledging each one of us for being here when this joyous event happened. Supper took longer than usual, everyone had second helpings, which says that supper was good, no one asked for desert after eating. We were filled, to the max and waited for a long time before settling for any deserts. We sat around the table talking and making plans for New Years Eve, Dawn went on the computer to see what was going on downtown for that night and if they were any good events, and called some of her friends to see where they were going.

After getting up from the table we took turns making sure all the left over's were put away before any other things were done. We sat and watched the football game that was on and changed channels to watch the college basketball game, but most of the evening was watching the football game between rivals, and always a good game for l their fans on this special day. The evening went by quite fast and after a couple hours we settled for desert, they were now some space for it. Everyone helped themselves to what they wanted, and returned to watch the game, after the game we sat and talked about the next major occasion, when it was going to take place, and where.

They were anxious for me to get married quickly but we told them there are things that were needed to be put in place before the wedding day is set. First Didi, has to see if there is any jobs job here doing exactly what she does, I have to look into it for her, as soon as that happens then we would set a date for the wedding, but not before, everything is settled and in placed.

After Dawn got off the computer it was decided to attend the best happening down town where the ball was dropping to ring in the New Year. Since that was solved we talked while washing the dishes and putting away. After doing that chore some of us needed a night snack, we had popcorn, and then waited a while before going off to bed. They were silence in the living room where they preferred to sleep, and from time to time they were giggling now and then, suddenly nothing, and we knew they were all asleep.

The morning arrived earlier than most days the sun was bright and the heat could be felt. It was breakfast, and l the children settled for cereal and toast and also some juice of their choice. I made breakfast for Didi and myself and since they were nothing on the agenda for the morning we chilled out until our guest arrived. It was getting to the time of their arrival, and everyone was dressed and looking smart then they was a knock on the door, Matt had the privilege of opening it and letting our guest's in with a warm welcome, with greetings of the season.

We sat down and chat for a long time sipping drinks and nibbling at finger foods which we prepared just for this occasion. The children got into chatting with Delores and Nick, asking a lot of questions which they answered. They were so glad for Didi and me when we told them, I had proposed to her, and she had accepted it with open arms. The evening was spent talking while Didi and Delores got acquainted with each other since she was used to her voice whenever she calls me at work.

Nick in the mean time was talking to the children telling them about his work, they listened attentively to every word he said, at times he told a told them a couple jokes, and had them laughing. The evening was well spent and had a good visit, with Delores, and Nick. It was time for them to leave they said good-bye thanked us for everything then they were out the door and off to her parents house. I made sure the door was locked for the night since we were not going anywhere again. The children were in a good mood, sat and watched television until they felt tired, and ready for bed.

All together it was a good day well spent talking and doing some eating which happens during this time of the year the only other times is Thanksgiving when families really get together and talked about the past year and what the coming year would bring them in the future. That no one is sure off, and would tell you the future is not a sure thing.

I laid in bed thinking about the day, and the coming days, what will the future be for me in the coming year, my thought were on Didi, looking at her and, the happy look on her face, while watching her ring. The only thing left at this moment is to relax and see what takes place in the New Year since it would be a new start in each our lives. My sleep did not come easy since I was tossing around, on the pillow at times, Didi was sound asleep, but was not disturbed anytime during my tossing, and turning.

The morning arrived though my sleep was uninterrupted awoke as if I had a good night sleep. The children were still sleeping so we stayed in bed for a while, because it was the day after Boxing Day. We waited until the children got up before starting breakfast, giving us more time to hold each other in bed. We heard the sound of laughter, and knew they were up, and ready to take on the day's challenge whatever they had planned among themselves.

We had breakfast, and the children got dressed, said they were going to the mall to see if they were any bargains, on that note decided accompanied them. They went their way and we did our thing, the mall was crowded with shoppers looking for the same things we were there for bargains. The time that we spent looking for bargains was very tiring, that it was not really worth the hassle, it was walking in to every store and comparing the price tag to see if the items had been reduced after the holiday sales.

Didi and I sat at the food court and waited for the children to finish their bargain hunt and looked tired carrying all they had bought both hands full of stuff. We helped them with some of their goods; it is amazing what children can find when they put their mind to do something. It was a couple hours after lunch time, and got into the car for home, taking everything out. The children sat on the floor showing us what they bought and how much it cost even Alex got himself some nice outfit for the beginning of the new school term.

While the children were showing us what they had brought the food was warming in the oven, as soon as it was ready it was placed on the table. We l ate buffet style everyone taking what they wanted and sat wherever they choose. It was a good idea because it saved time setting the table which made sense.

I could not believe the days were going so fast since Didi, and Alex arrived it seems as though it was yesterday they arrived. It has been eight day ago, soon the time would be getting shorter with each passing hour. The days are starting to get a little shorter and the nights longer because it is that time of the year when the winter solace begin. We have much to be thankful for, with all of us gathered together as a family, knowing that in the coming year if all goes well, they would be more time spent together.

After eating Dawn asked if Alex could go over where they lived and meet their mother, and I said yes he was happy to go out with them. We dropped them off, while Didi, and I went for a casual drive visiting various sites around town and the outskirts. We stopped at a few antique places to see what we could find but nothing caught our eyes, there was a big warehouse and lots of people were going in and out we stopped, and to my surprise it was a flea market. I never knew that this building were there almost everything your eyes ever laid sight on, a bargain hunters dream.

We purchased a couple small items, for her parents who collected special items, and then we drove home. The children did not call to say they were ready, so we stopped at a small cafe, had tea with some delicious pastries. We had just finished when the phone rang it was Matt, calling to say they were ready tò be picked up. It was another twenty minutes before we came to the house, looking out the window as the children came towards the car was Sarah, she wanted to see who was in the car with me.

It was most unusual to see that, all these years I was dropping the children home she had never looked out the window but today she did, out of curiosity. It was not a big problem for me but maybe for her, seeing that my son the children's brother was with them, at her house. The children were growing like weeds and getting older and wiser. Dawn would soon be turning eighteen years of age and was looking forward after graduation to attend university either at home or away. Matt on the other hand would be thirteen in about two months, and Alex would be turning seven years in a month.

This is fantastic within another year they would be a year older, so would I. My plans were to make sure they continue doing well in school, and help them in any way I can.

We returned home after a good days outing, had a little more left over's after it was reheated, we sat around the table, and nothing was left in any of the dishes or bowls. The clean up started with washing the dishes, and tidying the kitchen before sitting to relax and have any desert, something the children looked forward too. They l took turns saying what they wanted, each one came and get it in single file no one was short of what they requested, they were more than enough to go around twice.

It was time for the news to begin with the television on we sat and look to see what was happening, around our area locally. They were no sad news to talk about but the announcer said there would be some fun things happening for the children, which was free. The starting time was 8:00 pm, we got ready and drove down to the event and to make sure we got in the gate before the show started.

The show began right on time and the children started dancing when the first band on the concert roster started. They were three more bands to follow the first with a maximum play time of one hour and a half for each one. It was a great show bands that all of them knew from listening to them on the radio, and seeing their videos no television. The last band that came on stage was a popular band from here in California, playing most of their favourites, and it was good to see the children and Didi along with myself really having a good time dancing.

The concert was about coming to the end, and all the previous band members came back on stage and performed the singing of the National Anthem, before the crowd left for their homes. It was time for us to exit and return to our home, it was so much fun, if that is what took place tonight I would like to see if this could be out done on New Year's eve night when the ball is dropped.

It was unanimous that we stopped for a night cap we did at a soda fountain everyone had shakes of different flavours, to go home. We were all tucked out and tired, when we got home everyone got into night clothes, and turned into bed each one saying good night as though we were the Waldon house hold if some of you can remember the show on television.

The sun came up brighter than usual and can only mean one thing it would be hot today. Everyone was up and ready for breakfast, the children decided to make breakfast for a change giving Didi and I a chance to relax. It was good to see then working together not the first time. They made an omelette with all the veggies that they could find along with some ham, and sausages.

The smell of it being cook had my taste buds salivating, when it was all done we were call to the table, they did a wonderful job. After eating breakfast they let us know it was our turn to do dishes which we did gladly. The children was making plans for the day what they were going to do, they all came up with going to the movies. They looked in the movie section of the paper chose a movie they had not seen, and the time it was being shown, they got ready and went out the door on their way leaving us at home.

In another day or so it would be New Years, Didi and Alex would be leaving for Chicago, and had me thinking how lonely it would be. The sound of the children giggling or talking would be no longer but there would be more days to come hopefully in the coming months. It would be a sad day for all when that time comes but in the mean time we have to make the best of it together as the days gets shorter.

There is no time to be thinking about that day at this moment there are here with us enjoying themselves, I should be doing the same. What it came down to is am I having a good time. The answer is definitely a big yes, and was glad to have them spending the holidays here in California. We got ready because I wanted to show Didi my office and how far it was from home off we went, showing her my favourite places as we drove to the office, which was pleasant for this time of the day.

After viewing my office we stop at one of my favourite restaurant's and had something to eat, knowing that the children would not be ready to come home. We placed our order, and talked about a lot of things we had to change when we got married, and she come to California to live. It was something I was looking forward to, we would have to get a bigger house with four bedrooms each of them having their own room when they want quiet time or be alone. She was in total agreement, after eating we drove around some neighbourhood looking at houses to see what she liked that was near schools.

They were some houses she liked but were a little too far from the school Matt attended but thinks she would want Alex to attend but they would have to be a compromise when the time comes. It was just to have a feel for the surroundings and see what the neighbourhood looks like. On our way home we drove passed the house that we used to live in before our marriage ended, that she liked, but it was only three bedrooms.

It was getting late in the evening the phone rang Dawn ask if we could pick them up. We did on our way home called the pizza restaurant and ordered a couple large ones with their favourite they love, another with what Didi and I liked. It was waiting for us when we got there picked them up and drove home to enjoy our supper that consisted of pizza, and any drinks that were in the fridge.

The pizza was about finished except for a couple slices on each box, we were filled, and the rest was put away for anyone that wanted more to eat. It was suggested we play a board game before the news came on that we did it was fun to see us playing as a family and enjoying each other's company. The game finished in time the new was to coming on, looking at it made comments about what we saw as it was being presented to us over the air.

The news was always presented in ways that small children could understand, but when there is any violent news they do not show the pictures. This is good not only for parents but little children not having that kind of exposure to violence. We had not given any thought of what we were going to do after the news because the children went to a movie they did not want to see any. We sat and watched the college football being played on the sports channel.

The team with the first possession scored in the opening drive, and the other team had a hard time going down field. They were so many penalties in their first possession that they turn over the ball leading to a goal when the first half came around. The score was so lopped sided; we changed from that game to basketball, which was more fun watching. The game went into double overtime with the team having the last possession trying a long shot beyond the perimeter winning it by one point.

It was very close to bed time, and we had a light night snack before going to bed, the dishes were placed in the dish washer with the breakfast dishes to be done when we turned in for the night. The moon was up in the sky and shone bright, lighting up outside as though it was day, but everyone knew it was night, saying good night. We went to sleep, and hoped the morning will not come too quickly. My sleep was more peaceful than the other night when I tossed and turned, and was now interrupted by different thoughts.

At last morning came after having a good sleep, Didi was still asleep but the children were not, they were talking quietly amongst themselves trying not to wake us up, after several minutes she got up and also the children. They went to the bathroom one after another doing their morning hygiene, and then came out to see what was being made for breakfast, being the last day of the year. The next day was going to be hard for all Didi and Alex had to leave for Chicago in time so they can get themselves ready for work and school.

As the day progressed we did not think about what was happening the next day, we tried to make the best of the day that were at hand. Didi started some packing early because she did not want to rush, in case anything may be forgotten, and they get to the airport on time. We had to think about tonight spending New Year's Eve together as a family and bringing in the New Year with pleasant thoughts, and what we talked about for the pass weeks.

It was a lazy day spent by all no one wanted to do anything, at times the children would get together in a bedroom and talk with the door closed, carrying on a private conversation. It was nearing lunch time and we had some ham left, and made ham sandwiches with some cut up veggies. The mood was somber not much talking a few tears trickling down the children faces, but they were glad to meet Alex and Didi but very sad to see them leave.

The mind set was not doing any cooking for supper either I said for tonight we are going to order Chinese food and eat before leaving for the New Year's celebration down town. All was in favour the order was placed and the time it has to be delivered; in the mean time we sat talking about what we were going to do in the New Year that would make it enjoyable for all.

The invitation went out to Alex that he could come for March break if he had one, he said sure, and promised him one of us would come to Chicago to be on the plane with him, and I would take him back but both children wanted to go so I said ok. Didi said when the time came she would pick them up at the airport.

Just after talking the door bell rang and right away we knew the food had arrived, I paid the driver, and then it was time to have our supper. This was a special New Year's Eve dinner on a special occasion. We got the plates, and utensils out, and sat down to eat, cleaned up the kitchen and got ready for the drive downtown. I knew that there would be traffic jams so we left early to beat the rush and to get a good parking spot.

You could hear a pin drop in the car, it was so quiet the only time it changed was when Didi and I asked a question and a reply was given, other than that it was sheer silence. The traffic was not bad going downtown but it was expected to be worst going home some of the people would come in late for the dropping of the ball and the final ending to see the fireworks the last one for the year.

The parking was free for all because we reached early we got a good parking spot which was easy to get out. We found our way close to the event where we would be able to see every action that was taking place on the stage. It was a good thing we brought windbreakers as the night air was a bit chill, not so much for Didi, and Alex being from the far north this was mild in comparison to what they are used to.

The show started on time but the music was not like the one we saw a week ago, this one was a bit lousy. Since we were here stayed until the next band came on stage with more of an upbeat tempo and had everyone tapping their foot, and dancing along to the sweet music being played. It was better now that the action was getting into full swing, more people started trickling in and before we knew it the place was packed.

Everyone was having a great time right up to the time they announced the time was getting close to count down of the New Year's ball drop. The music continued right up to a minute before the time came for the countdown. The ball started dropping right at the stroke of midnight, the song Olde Lang Syne started and everyone that knew the song started singing bringing in the New Year, everyone wishing each other a happy New Year.

Driving home turned out to be hectic lots of traffic jam it was expected, because of the amount of people that were there witnessing the dropping of the New Year's ball. The time spent in traffic gave us time to talk about the holidays and asking questions if it was a good one well spent, every one said yes even to the point of getting to know both Alex and Didi it was well worth them being here with us. That made me feel good hearing the two elder children saying those words was assuring not only for me but also Didi and Alex.

We make it home just before 1:00am on this the first day of the New Year, when everyone got into the house we made our own toast having non alcohol drink wishing everyone a Happy New Year. The time came for everyone to go to bed because we had to get up early have breakfast, and take Didi and Alex to the air port. We said good night and went to bed; Didi on the other hand could not sleep squeezing my hand she said! I would like you to make love to me, and we started to caressed each other until the passion and ecstasy with the adrenaline rush getting the better of us then the gyration of the waist and the insertion of my penis into her vagina it brought her to a sweet climax and at the same time she had orgasm I had mine.

The sex was good for both it was sort of a good bye symbol to each other until me meet again, soon after we both fell asleep. The next morning we all got up as the sun was rising, it was good to see everyone getting themselves ready to have breakfast and get out the door on our way to the airport. The departure time was 11:00 am California time which is at least three or four hours behind Chicago's this would get them home when there is still some light.

It was a sad day not only for me but, for all mostly the children, especially Dawn s had gotten closer to her little brother and the bond they shared for one another was that great, it would have an effect on all the children. The first to say good-bye was Matt, then Dawn who cried when she hugged Alex, and Didi she could not help it she said; it was just one of those days. I was last to say good-bye giving Alex a hug telling him I would keep in touch, then it was Didi's turn with a squeeze and a kiss she replied in her sexy voice I Love You! Then both went through the gates to their plane waving as they went on their way

We drove home after the plane took off no one spoke for a while then the silence was broken when I said how about stopping to get something to eat. They both agreed, and wanted a burger fries and a drink. I had chicken with fries; we talked about the whole holidays experience having about Didi, and Alex then Dawn looked at me with those sad eyes but did not cry. The conversation was changed to another topic this time it was about school, and if they were ready to get back into studying again.

The house was very quiet they were no laughter, just the occasional giggle when they both remember some funny joke they shared with Alex. It was hard on me also knowing that we were here as a family, and now we were back to just me and the children, sometime in the next coming months that would change. I knew what I had to done the planning would be after making a phone call to my friend who owes me a huge favour.

The children went into their room, and took a nap because they had gotten up early; I did the same, and got up when the phone rang. It was Didi, letting us know they arrived home safe, Dawn came out when she heard me talking, asked: who was it, and asked if she can to talk to Alex. She did before saying good bye told him she love him then pass the phone to me, Didi and I spoke for a few minutes more then said good-bye.

It was getting late, supper was started, so the children could eat before taking them home, in that way they could get their books ready for school. I kept thinking about ways of getting things done faster than normal as supper was being prepared, but it may be kind of impossible to do. I would have to really pull some strings to make it happen, I dropped the idea about the whole thing letting nature takes its own course.

The things they wanted for supper was done sat down to eat, and the children ask me when I was going to get married. My answer was I have to wait to hear from a friend of mine. I am owed a huge favour and tomorrow during work I will make a call to see if he can expedite the favour he owes me. I will both of you know sometime during the week t, hopefully it would turn out to be positive, and we all would be happy.

The children got ready to be dropped off at their home, checking around to see if they had forgotten any items they would needed for school. We left after everything was ok. I returned home to an empty house and to dead silence you could hear a pin dropped from any room. I did not feel like doing much, I read the newspaper, and then continued reading a book that was started a while back before the holidays began.

Before going to bed I watched television for an hour then turned in, the night was going to be long for me since it's the first night not having Didi, by my side. Although it felt good having her here it felt worst not having her next to me tossing and turning throughout the night I finally fell asleep. The morning sun was shining through the window and into my eyes, and awoke to the sound of the birds chirping loud as though some thing was arousing them, and it was. They was a cat walking by the nest they had built in the tree nearby.

The drive to the office was somber, that was something I had to live with for a while, knowing some day we would be together for good. I am a lucky man to have her by my side instead of sulking not having her here with me at this moment. I entered the building went to my office waited patiently for the office staff to arrive and wish them a Happy New Year. My hope for this year was everything that we planned at work is fulfilled and more.

One by one the office staff trickled into the office and they were a certain glow on some of their faces, which was good to see meaning they had a very good holiday. Delores came in and stopped by my office to say hello and wish me a happy New Year, and asked if Didi and Alex got away on time and safely at home. The conversation was a pleasant one; she left for her office when everyone was in placed at their desks. I came out wished everyone present a happy New Year, and then went to the rest of the floors doing the same.

After returning from wishing everyone on each floor that we occupied I made a call to Didi, just to hear her voice, making sure she was ok. She was, and at the same time the ring was being showed off because some of the staff notice a glow in her eyes, which they had never seen before. They were happy for her, some even said they knew something was going on between the two of us for a while but was not sure until now. I said bye to her and she said good bye too, and got back to work.

The day was moving very slowly being the first working day of the new year usually do, but as the month ends the days seems to accelerate without slowing down. I made a call after lunch to my friend that owes me a huge favour. I explained the situation to him, and said he would get back to me in the next couple days. In the mean time he mentioned to have Didi, sent him her resume, another call was made to her giving her all the details that he needed.

The day ended on a positive note, I got an email from my friend saying he would be opening another office in the next coming months, and would need someone with a good business sense, and that was good to hear. This was good to hear driving home they were high hopes that something would happen soon. I made a call to Didi, and told her what was relayed to me, making her even happier but we would have to wait and see if the job materialized.

The weeks came and went by without any words then suddenly he called to tell me the office was going to be moving forward. He said an email was sent to Didi asking her how soon she could be here, soon after hearing from him my phone rang. That voice I knew said! guess what? And I said what; she said she would be there as soon as she books a flight, within a week. I was happy for her which means if all goes according plans there could be a wedding in the near distance.

Monday morning came, without fail, the start of another week is just beginning, and I am starting to hate the first day of work because the weekends felt so short. You really do not have enough time in to do anything for yourself. I passed by the restaurant, grabbed some breakfast to take with me, sitting at my desk eating it the phone rang, it was Didi, calling to let me know she would be down on the Friday. I was in a happy mood; she would be here for the weekend, and leaving the Tuesday on the midday flight back to Chicago. I was happier now knowing she would be here with us for a couple days again. My day was kept busy with Delores bringing me memos and letters to sign that had to be mailed before the day ended.

The week ended on a very positive note today being Friday Didi was arriving this evening, and was about to leave for the airport because, the plane was going to be; landing within the hour. I decide to wait until she arrived to get something to eat. The plane landed on schedule and when it was announced my heart skipped a couple beats for sheer joy once again the love of my life was here within the space of a month.

I saw her before she entered the waiting, and the smile on the face explained it all she was happy to be back. She never thought it was going to happen that fast, having very good friends and many contacts it was time to ask favours. I was glad she did not have supper as yet taking her bags from her we headed straight to the car, then a restaurant to get something to eat. I did not tell the children she was coming, I asked how was Alex doing, she said fine mom and dad send their regards to you. I wanted it to be a surprise when the children came over later, after their school activities.

The weekend was looking great from where I was sitting, with smiles all over my face it was not hard to see why it was? With me holding her hands before supper arrived assured me she was really here in person. Our supper was served and the two of us sat and watched each other as we ate. I called Dawn, and Matt to see if they wanted me to pick them up from school and they said sure. We did and the look on their face when they saw Didi was one of shock and happiness all at the same time.

They were so happy to see her they both hugged her at the same time and without failed they asked about Alex, and Dawn was glad to know he was doing well. On the way home the children asked her what she was doing back here, when she told them they were even happier, and said we hope you get the position. We really do miss you both since you left; it was not the same because we had just started to know you and next thing it was time for you to leave.

Home sweet home at last we went into the house, me carrying the bags, taking it straight to my room where she would be sleeping. We sat down and relaxed, talked about what was Alex up to then remembered she promised to call him at her parents' house when she got in. She called and the voice said hello she knew immediately who it was, hi mom! Hi son! She said my trip was good then he asked about Dawn, and Matt, and his dad they are all fine, can I talk to them sure, hold for a minute! We all talked to him before he said his good- byes.

The weekend is shaping up to be a great one Didi is here with us truthfully with me. She is here on a job interview. If it turns out she gets the position she would have some decision what to make about her job at our Chicago office. It is not a decision that can be made on the spur of the moment but I would really want her and Alex here with me and the kids, it is a decision she alone can make with a little help from me, and see how it turn out.

The decision is hers, I can only guide, and help get whatever monies she has coming by way of a severance package for the time she has been working at the office in Chicago. It is a lot to process, if the job that she may be offered has a good outcome. We sat around chatting having tea along with some pastries, this was a good time as any to say welcome back, and hope the next time we see you here it would be for good.

The flight to California was a bit tiring Didi excused herself, went into the bedroom changed into something comfortable then returned. She did not stay for any length of time within a half an hour said good night, the children and I remained talking a bit longer before turning into bed. The moment I walked into the bedroom, she looked at me, with her arm stretched, said come to me my love. I went forward into those arms where she gave me a gentle hug and kisses, for being who I am.

They were no hesitation on my part with those out stretched arms who can resist that call, it was more than just come here, and it was a call for a little action. By action meaning one thing she wanted was to have sex tonight, the tempo was upbeat without batting an eye we were over each other. The next thing was our clothes were scattered on the floor my penis was into her vagina with an in and out movement until we came to a climax giving way to an orgasm with the feeling of sheer joy.

The night started out great sex, which was both our intention and lots of love you before falling asleep. I must say she is one woman I know when she wants something she get it. I am glad the person she is getting all that love from is me, and no other. I am going to stop here, say good night because I need to get some shut eyes tomorrow being another day, with more activities to be done.

I had a good night sleep after having sex with a special person, the morning gave me new hope someday that special person would be here with me and the children for good, now I would concentrate on the here and now. If it is needed at this time I have to make the best of it. The children were still asleep, so was Didi, but I had to get up and have a tea before they awake and start asking what are we having for breakfast, and what were the plans for today.

I know one think groceries had to be done, what the children wanted to do after, was not on my mind when they get up they would tell me what plans they have for the rest of the day. I heard Didi calling, so I called back letting her know was in the dining room having a tea. She came out joined me, wanting to know what we were doing after breakfast. I told her some shopping she looked excited for the first time she would be going grocery shopping with the children and me.

I started preparing breakfast our Saturday morning special, when the children smell the bacon; they woke up dashing to do their bathroom routine. They came out ready to eat, during the conversation at the table they ask what was happening today, Didi told them and they said cool! They had never gone shopping with her before. It is their opportunity to do so, and have an idea what she is like shopping as a future stepmother.

The day went fast after shopping, and putting the groceries away, the children wanted to go for a hike so we headed to our favourite place. The children liked that area ever since they were small, and was one of the places they visit frequently with me. I am proud to know they like the outdoors like I do; now Didi would have to get use to the Saturday hikes with us. Giving her some time she would fit in when she gets accustom with our Saturday routine, all this can change providing everything works out in her favour after the job interview on Monday.

The day was well spent having fun as we walk, talking to each other; we stopped at our favourite spot for something to eat. It was not long after eating we saw an accident not too far up from the place we were eating luckily they were no fatality. We passed the accident scene with caution, and drove home very carefully. I pulled into the drive said thank the Lord! We sat around the table for a while before we got together and started preparing supper, and planning Sunday's supper.

The supper was all prepared but the chicken had to be placed in the oven to be baked, along with the vegetables around it. The next couple hours we sat watching television until supper was ready; when it was ready the table was set with the plates and utensils. After the chicken came out of the oven we l sat down to have supper. It was not the first time we fixed supper together that was done over the Christmas holidays, when Alex was here with us as a family.

We all awoke early next day for church, mass was at 8:30 am our usual time. We sat in the middle of the church, when the parishioners came in they watch us as they went by thinking in their mind who was that person sitting in the pew with us. I did not pay any attention to them but concentrate on what was going on at the front of the church alter with what the priest was saying during his sermon for today.

After the mass was over I introduced Didi to the priest, he was impressed with the way she presented herself. I know he wanted to ask me a question or two because of the amount of parishioners that was exiting he did not. We left headed over to where we always had Sunday breakfast, and had to be wait to be seated today of all days they were busy. We were called after five minutes, looking at the menu to see what we were going to order my eyes glanced in the corner where the judge and his wife were seated their usual corner having breakfast.

The judge's wife eyes were on me all the time she was eating if that stare could kill I would be dead right there on the spot. I made no mention of it to anyone at the table, but continued eating glancing at their table from time to time to see what she was up to. After they had finished eating they both came across to say hello, Didi was introduced to them, and her face showed a bit of disgust when she saw the ring on Didi's finger giving her the sign from here on this man is off limits to anyone.

They both left after talking, soon after our bill came it was paid we left for home. The morning was just coming to an end and soon it would be noon. We all had a late breakfast decided to sit around reading the newspaper, it would be a while before we had to prepare supper, and so we continued reading and talking from time to time. The time to start preparing supper was creeping up on us; getting up started the preparation of the various dishes we were going to have, then the rest of the gang joined in helping where they can.

The supper took some time before it was ready, the children set the table, and as soon as it was ready we sat down to have dinner, to complete supper we had deserts each having something different. The table was cleared the e dishes washed and put away, before the children got busy doing their homework, which had to be handed in the next day.

The two of us sat on the couch reading the papers while the children continued with their homework, with few questions asked. It was very quiet with the occasional whispering at times. The news would soon be coming on as the children were doing their work we went inside to watch the news, giving them quiet time to concentrate and complete it without having to be disturbed by what was happening on television.

The news had just ended and, the children had also completed their homework, and started putting their books away. They said they would be ready for home within the hour, when they get themselves ready. The signal was given they were ready, they gave Didi a hug and told her good bye wishing her good luck tomorrow; Didi did not go with me she had some clothes that needed ironing for her interview tomorrow.

After the children got dropped off I took a drive to see how long it would take me to drop Didi off for her interview, or she could have the car and keys for the apartment. I returned home after the drive and told her that she would have the car tomorrow for the interview it was an easy drive and not too far from where I work. It was the best thing, she could come back and get me after I am through working, she agreeded since the drive was on a straight road.

The problem about her driving me to work was settled, what are we going to do presently knowing the children is not here. We relaxed, and talked about what to expect on the interview, with that out of our system held hands while talking about whatever came to minds. The night was still in its early stages that were before 9:00pm, we watched a movie on television until we felt tired and ready for bed. We, walked hand in hand entered the b bedroom changed clothes and went to bed. It was early rising, had breakfast and Didi dropped me off to work and she proceeded to her interview.

This morning was different than most only it was now two of us having to get ready at the same time, while Didi was getting ready me was preparing breakfast. In this way when she is out and dressed I can do my thing while she had her breakfast. She looked very stunning this morning something I have never seen before, she had dressed to impress it shows she cared about the way she looks, giving that positive impression at the interview.

We left the house in sufficient time for her to drop me off to work, while she continued for her interview. The interview was at 9:30 am giving her time to relax and think about the questions she may be asked, after the interview she came by the office to see me. What I saw on her face it seems as though it went well. At this point all eyes were on her as she walked in, introduced her to everyone on my floor, at the same time Delores came out to see what the commotion was about, and was very much surprise to see her again so quickly.

After introducing her to the staff she came back to my office, and talked about the interview, and all that took place, saying that it felt good, at the same time very positive about her chances of being offered the job. She left for home, and told her when I needed to be picked up I would call she said that's great! Then she left. I returned to my office and continued doing my work but was interrupted by a phone call from my friend telling me there is a good chance she would get the job, but was not to tell her anything as yet, good I promised, I would not say a word to her.

My friend said he would send an email informing her of being approved for the position, and she would have to start in the next four months. This would give her enough time to settle things with her previous employer, with that said I continued working. I had a smile on my face while working up to the time before she picked me up. I took her out for supper, because she had a good day, and was proud of her for coming on such short notice for the interview.

I took her to a special place of her choice where we can sit in a booth and have some privacy together with no prying eyes. We held hands before the menu came and after, before the food came I gave her a kiss, she asked what that was for, simple told her because I love you.

She was going home tomorrow to get an email stating that she got the job, knowing her would call me the minute she see it. I have to be straight face without letting her know I knew the answer all along. The evening turned out to be a beautiful just us in a booth where no eyes can penetrate our every movement. The food was delicious and we enjoyed it, along with the food she had a glass of wine to end the evening, and I a glass of non alcoholic drink, when it was finished and the bill was paid, we left for home.

The phone rang just as we entered the house it was Dawn, she wanted to ask Didi how the interview went. I left them talking to each other, went inside to change my clothes before sitting to watch the evening news on television. It was a daily ritual I have being doing for quite a long time, always wanting to know what was happening in the city or the surrounding neighbourhoods.

Didi and Dawn chatted for a while, when she was finished came and sat with me as the news was being shown, it is something I can get used to again with someone by my side. I am very much looking forward to her and Alex being here, but it may be hard to leave her parents there in Chicago. Me knowing her parents they would want her to take the job and move to a warmer climate knowing she can still visit where she would always be welcome.

She made a call to her parent's home letting them know that the interview went well, and she would be home tomorrow. She spoke to Alex who was glad to hear her voice. He said hi to me then went back to doing whatever he was doing, she continued talking to her parents for another half hour before saying good night to them both.

I think she was happy to be here at the same time happy to be going home to a place she knew all her life except when she was in university here in California, where we first met. She was in her first year and me in my third year. It was lots of fun with her and dreamt some day we were going to get married, and here we are making that dream a reality, who would have thought all these years it would have happened to the both of us this way. It was a long day today and she had to get a good night sleep for her trip tomorrow. We turned in, with the lights off and our bodies next to each other that the spark we had ignited and we became hotter and had to quench the flame somehow, led to having sex to douse our burning flames and having it extinguished.

We both got up as the morning sun began rising, getting ready early, relaxed, while having breakfast, she got ready for the airport, while the dishes were being washed and put away. She came out wearing a pair of jeans with a white top that looked very stunning. She had me taking a second look, as she twirled her figure showing lots of curve which I knew she had but was never displayed like what I was seeing.

It was time for us to leave, taking her bags to the car drove out of the entrance onto the road and into the flow of traffic, taking the thruway straight to the airport, and most of the traffic was going the opposite direction it was easy going. We reached and she checked in, we sat around talking her flight was announced, gave each other a big hug and kiss, then on her way through the gate to board her plane.

As the plane took off I headed for work, the day was long but waited to hear from her when she got home. I worked a little later since getting to work late putting in some extra time, something that was usually done today was one of those days. I waited for a while then the phone rang it was Didi all very excited, when she opened her email. She could not believe the interview she had on Monday that the job was a sure thing, and they wanted to know if I would be able to start in four months.

That was no surprise I had already knew the answer, but acted surprised, she had the time to think about what she was going to do. She have to act as soon as possible before the owner change his mind, with a loud shriek said, she would accept the position, and would be making plans to come to California to be there with me. In the mean time she said, I have to tell mom, dad, and Alex he would really like to get to see his sister and brother all the time.

She hung up the phone after saying love you, soon after that conversation left for home. I was glad for her; now that everything was finalized it would not be too long for us to start planning our wedding day. It is something we have been waiting for all these years, and now that it is happening we have to make the best of both worlds. The phone rang again Didi said to me! When do you want to get married, as soon as we can set a date I would gladly marry you, and have you as my wife Ok! She said will get back to you with the answer click! That was it she was gone in an instant.

Now that she has accepted the job offer, she would have to be here in California for two weeks at a time, making sure the offices are set up the way she wants it, and have a good flow for everyone. I am sure she would do a splendid job because she is good at whatever she does, making whoever she works for the company would be very profitable in its endeavour.

I am beginning to accept the fact she would be here at times, and house hunting would have to start soon, without her until she arrives. I would have to keep my eyes open for any houses coming on the market in a neighbourhood that Didi, would like, which would be not too far from the school Matt attends.

It was bedtime, and while laying on the bed thought about every possible date we could set for our wedding, before I knew it sleep came, the next morning it took me a while to get going. I did happen to be at work on time although it was a long stop getting my breakfast to go. The lineup was long and seems as though the line was not moving at the drive through. I read some memos after having my breakfast, the phone rang, it was Adam, my friend who gave the job to Didi, and he wanted to know how she was doing, when she opened her email informing her of the position.

I told him she was fine, and he should be getting an email from her very soon with her answer. He was pleased with her answers, and brought a lot of insight with her experience, and what she would like happened when she starts working. After that call it made me feel good knowing he had high regards for her.

I started working again without interruptions for awhile Delores, knocked at the door entered, and wanted to talk to me about something that was bothering her. I sat and listened while she talked, what was on her mind, giving her some much needed advice about her problems. She wanted to get a man's view on things she was going through with Nick. She left when some of her questions were answered she was looking for; based on what I told her she said thanks for the advice. It seems they were lots of things bothering her, and had someone to vent her problems, without judging her base on what she was saying about her boyfriend. I am glad the talk we had was helpful to her at this point.

Today it seems was a day for people to get things off their minds, and was grateful to be there, and listen with an open mind; home was looking good at this time, where I can just relax, having some quiet time all to myself. I did not prepare anything for supper but settled for some cold cereal, and toast which went down very good.

I started reading today for the first time, did not watched the news, but kept reading the book that I had started a while back, trying to complete it before going to bed. Trying to concentrate and read was hard, lots of images were going through my mind, with Didi accepting the job here in California, and having to look for a house, that everyone would be comfortable, in the neighbourhood where we decide to live.

Sleep evaded me for a while when it did arrived, it was like a gust of wind with such a force dropping everything that was being done. As my head rest on the pillow my eye closed, and awoke next morning feeling great, got myself ready for work, and had breakfast and out the door. I did not stop for breakfast, but pickup a tea in the building cafeteria at work.

Today was going to be a good day, because of the great sleep I had, it was the last day of the week before the week end. The days started accelerating a little faster and so was the month it was coming down to the end of the first month of the New Year. Thinking to myself in a couple weeks it's Alex's birthday, and would have to send him a card. I also want to surprise the both of them on his birthday. I made plans to fly to Chicago a day before to celebrate it with him and be back home in time for work on Monday morning.

I did not call Didi; the following week, booked my flight for early Friday afternoon, to arrive there before they went to bed. I rented a car when I checked out called, and told her I was in town and would be there shortly, she sound so happy I came, and asked her not to tell Alex anything. I knocked at the door, he opened it, and was happy to see me, hugged me so tight and did not want to let go.

He released me and walked me to the living room where his mother was sitting, standing, gave her a hug, then a kiss then sat next to her. It was a surprise to her but mostly Alex who wanted to know what I was doing in Chicago. I came to celebrate your birthday, now that you are turning eleven years of age. I would not want to miss it, this is the only time you would ever be eleven.

He said good night to us went to his bed room for the rest of the night. Didi and I talked for a while about setting a month for our wedding, but could not think of a date, but will try again before leaving Chicago early Monday morning. We turned into bed and thought what we were doing for Alex birthday, she mentioned go-cart racing, after there we would go over to her parents, have supper, and some of his friends from school would come over to celebrate his birthday one he would never forget.

The sun came up bright Saturday, drove him out to the go-cart tracks, and did not need to dress warm since it was indoors. He climbed into the car after he was given some instructions and off he went. He looked, as though he was doing this for quite a while, but it was his very first time. I was surprised as well as Didi how well he handled the circuit with the speed he was going, hardly bumping into the side trails.

The fun was over after two hours, we drove to the mall, where he chooses his birthday gift from me. I was expecting him to choose something big; he wanted a kindle to read books he liked. It was good he likes reading that was all he wanted, and came with a six subscription supply of books he could read whenever he chooses.

We had a small snack to eat, and then proceed to his grandparents' house for supper and a surprise party after, which he knew nothing about. It was kept very secret at school his friends did not tell him anything although they were at school with him every day. I watched his face when they keep walking into the house, beginning around 4:30 pm. The door to the basement was closed, he did not even venture to see why it was close; if he had, the party decorations would have been discovered and his birthday would not have been a surprise.

The children that were invited started strolling in one after the other the look on his face was one of shock. We heard him say to one of his friends, how come you did not say anything to me? It was suppose to be a secret. At this time Alex accepted what was happening, they had a great time together as though they were in school, having fun. After they had finished talking and he opened the gifts the birthday cake came out. The children along with the adults sang happy birthday to him, followed by cake and ice cream topping off the evening. The party was over after 8:00pm; everyone said good night and thanked us for inviting them.

We had a good night sleep until 7:00am Sunday morning; we got ready for church and had breakfast at a restaurant before returning home. It was a good hearty and healthy with lots to eat mostly buffet style, and we had quite a bit to ea. After our breakfast we drove home, changed into some comfortable clothes and relaxed reading the papers, Alex concentrate on his homework, asking for help the occasionally.

We did not talk about the month or day for our wedding while relaxing but wrote possible month, and day. We exchanged what each one had written down; it happened that we choose the same month but different day. The month was settled now we have to talk about the day, and I am hoping we can get that settled before the morning. I was sure we could come up with a day before returning to California in the morning, and just as I was about to get something to snack on, said, how about June 17th, why I ask? Well for one thing its fathers' day.

The month and the day were finalized, and I can have a good night's sleep, before heading home. The next morning got ready before Alex awoke had something to eat, drink, and said good-bye to them and out the door. I drove to the airport knowing the month, and day was set, and I can start putting things in motion, but had to a wait until Didi came to choose the invitations layout she liked.

I arrived at the airport with time to spare, checked in early and sat in the longue reading the papers before the plane departed. All the time thinking of the date we set for our wedding father's day above all things, this was going to be a day I would never forget which would be memorable.

The plane took off on time and would be landing on time in California. It was taxing down the tarmac ten minutes before it was scheduled to land giving me time to grab my breakfast to go. I was at the office before any staff arrived, while eating the phone rang, Didi was on the other end. She received a call from her new employer asking, if she could be here next week, and wanted me to know she would be down the following Sunday, and asked me to pick her on her arrival.

The office staff had just started coming in when I finished talking continued eating before starting work. At the end of the day's work drove by the realtor's office to view any houses that were for sale in the neighbourhood she liked. There was one that just came on the market with the amount of rooms, yard space and the price was right. I asked the real estate agent if they were any chance of me having a look at the inside. I left with him, drove over to the house and it was just what I had expected, well kept, and everything in great condition, even the appliances was up to date.

I picked her up from the airport that Sunday, and drove by the house the for sale the sign was not up as yet because I told the realtor not to do so until he heard from me. It was no surprise when she said she liked it, a lot since it was closer to the school Alex might be attending with his brother. I think Didi was sold on the house; I promised to call the realtor and asked him if we can view the house again this time with Didi.

I got dropped off at work early today and started working on some papers that needed my undivided attention to be completed. I got a call from Didi, saying they wanted her to stay for another week. I could not be happier, but she would have to use up some of her vacation that was due to her. I call her office in Chicago, informing them she would be here for another week, and they said fine. As I was getting back to work the phone rang, this time it was the realtor, and asked him if we can view the house again. There was someone who wanted to look at it he said sure, and told him we would meet him there but will call with the time.

After work Didi picked me up and drove by the house the realtor was there waiting on us, because I called and gave him the time. As we walked inside she was blown away by the way it was kept, and without any hesitation said I love it this is it. We started negotiation about the price, but would have to get my condo apartment sold.

He told me it was no problems and knew someone who was looking for a condo in the same neighbourhood mine was in. I told him ok and the price I wanted for mine, said he would talk to the prospective buyer. The house situation was soon to be settled, we put in an offer, which was accepted, on the condition that we sold ours, within a week of talking to the realtor my condo was sold, and bought the house.

We had two months to move, the other thing that needed to be taken care off was the invitation design. We called a printer who came to the Condo one afternoon, and with Dawn and Matt sat looking over the different designs. It was time for the children to get involve with our wedding plans, Didi wanted Dawn to be her maid of honour, she accepted, and Matt, was my best man after all who would make the perfect one but him, and Alex as the ring bearer.

They were three things left to be taken care of before Didi left for home. The next morning after dropping her off to work I made a couple calls to the caterers. The hall rental, was next and the last on the list was the D J who would be playing the music for us. The date we gave was great they did not have any one booked we were penciled in all was taken care of. The only thing we had to worry about was packing for our move in the next couple months.

Didi was leaving for Chicago next day, we were glad everything worked out before she left. She had to return and start making plans for when she could start her new job in California. It means leaving her parents and many friends' made over the years. It is one of the hardest things to do especially when you have to leave family behind you love so dearly, but on the other side they can spend winters with us when it becomes cold and unbearable.

I took her to the airport next morning, while driving said she was the luckiest person in the world to have met me, and said likewise. I parked the car and walked her into the airport, checked in her baggage, and spent some time talking; her flight was announced and gave each other a hug, and kiss. She walked through the gate to her plane, and left after the plane took off, then was off to work like everybody else.

Every day after work I did some packing, on the weekends the children helped. They were glad the move was a little closer to them. The house was only a few block, away in walking distance to school, and home, all items had to be packed before the end of

March. It was our moving dead line, the new owners wanted to move in by that time. We did what we could and each day a little more was packed.

The appliances at the Condo were staying since they were new ones at the house; the first week in March school was out for a one week break. The children decided to go over at the house to start cleaning, and painting the rooms with the colour of their choice. The phone rang Didi was at the other end, said that Alex, and I were on our way down for the week he was off. I met them as usual at the airport and drove home; both changed into comfortable clothing, and went over to the house doing any chores that needed doing.

The children were there already, we picked up some wings, pizza and drinks and they could eat whenever they were hungry. The rooms looked great after it was painted only the children's room was done that day. We left our room for last along with the living room, dining room, and kitchen. We could not decide on the colour to paint the living room. We took a picture of the couch t we bought and got the paint which suited the living room and would blend in with the surroundings.

The last three day that was left the children went out together leaving. I went to work; Didi stayed at home, one day decided she and the children would go hiking and pick me up on their return. It was good to see she was getting used to the surroundings, later she would have to know her way around the area.

The evening after eating supper we sat and type up address labels, applying them to the invitations that had to be mailed, before Didi returned to Chicago. It was lots of pressure on us but got the job done. The next day we went out, and left the children at home. I wanted to spend some time with her alone we drove to a park and walked around the pond holding hands. It was getting late and soon it would be supper time, I called home, told them we were bring home Chinese food for supper.

Then after supper we relaxed Didi and Alex was leaving the next day around midday for Chicago. Alex looked sad he did not want to leave. He was having a good time with his brother and sister but knew he would be here when the new school term begins. He was not looking forward to going back but understood he would have to finish his term there before returning to live in California. A couple weeks after they returned Didi called to tell me they had found a replacement for her, and she was packing things up, and getting ready to move. The movers would be coming to do all the packing in the next couple days.

The next couple days when she called, you could hear the voice of a happy person and was finally moving to where her new job was, and where she would be living for a long time with the man she always loved, along with all the children together. I was glad t everything worked out and was able to help her in any way I could.

The day for moving her things here had arrived, she called to say the truck was on its way said bye to me a soft voice that sounded sad. It was sad, she was leaving her parents, and son behind for a completely new environment totally different from what she was used to. They would be changes not only for her but all of us in some way, although we were together this time it would be permanent.

The plane landed at the time she said it was going to, the children came with me to meet her, but without Alex. They knew he was coming after school Dawn asked if she could go with Didi to Chicago when she was going to bring him back, and I said sure. She was happy to be going, she had never been to Chicago before, and she now has the opportunity to do so when that time came. We were waiting for her to show up with the luggage she came with, it was not a lot just some that she can get by with.

At last she showed up dressed in a pair of jeans and a white sweater, holding a winter coat over her arm. The weather was cold when I left she said, while I am here there is no need for it. The only time I would need it is, when I visit my parents during one Christmas. We loaded her luggage into the car headed home stopping along the way at one of our favourite restaurants for something to eat, being close to supper time. It would be another two weeks before Didi started working at her new job because she sold her car she had to get a new one, which she choose, and liked because it suited her.

We called Alex to see how he was doing, but he was not at home. His grandmother answered the phone, and said he was out with his grandfather, and was doing well. In the following weeks both Dawn and Matt celebrated their birthdays making them a year older. I could hardly believe my eyes; they are growing up so fast.

We have heard from most of the people t we sent invitation to, that would give us a good idea how many guests t would be attending the wedding and also the reception. The thing we did not consider was hiring a wedding planner for decorating the hall, we thought we could do it ourselves, but changed our minds, and hire a decorator that was recommended to us.

The priest was contacted again, and wanted to see us about the date of the wedding, also to remind us about rehearsals. We went over that evening to see the priest, and talked about what he was expecting from us as a donation to the church. The next day the moving van pulled up into the drive way that had Didi's things she wanted to keep. It was placed into the basement where it could sorted later, and put them where they might fit.

The two weeks t Didi had when she arrived has now ended, she has settled in her new job. I am glad she is here with us while, they are other things that have to be taken care of the one thing t we did not let pass us was spending time together. I know that some days would be spent working longer hours than some, that would be expected of her since she is fully in charge of the new office.

The house is finally completed all the furniture's are in placed where we want them, the children are happy the way the house look especially their rooms, and the painting they did. It was time to sit and enjoy every part of the house knowing everyone was happy with the outcome. The only person missing was Alex, but would be joining us in another couple of weeks when Didi and Dawn goes to Chicago for a weekend to bring him back. I am looking forward to see him again the last time I saw him was on his birthday.

The weeks went by fast and were now mid May on Friday Didi and Dawn would be leaving for Chicago to bring Alex home. I know it would be comforting to him when he gets here in a way, and sad to leave his grandparents he practically grew up with. All hearts would be heavy for a while but it is not to say they would not be in touch with each other on a constant basis.

The time came for Matt and me to pick up the gang at the airport, it was an emotional one for me knowing that Alex has come home, and would be with us for a long time. The plane touched down on time but took a while to get to the gate, because of another plane was late leaving from that gate; it was l due to a late passenger arrival.

He looked so grown up when he exited, dressed in cargo pants and a sweatshirt. He walked as though he owned the place, when he laid eyes on us ran as fast as he could forgetting who he had came with. I gave him a great big hug and jumped on Matt, giving him a tight hug, and for a moment I thought he was not getting down.

The entire luggage was accounted for we load them into the car he said; it is good to be in California. The wedding day are getting closer with each tick of the clock, there were some things left to be done. The most important part was taken care of, the dresses and the tuxedos had to be looked after, after taking a rest, the following Wednesday we went separate ways to get fitted, and meet home when all fittings were finished.

The entire wedding was now a go with the dresses fitted to suit, and the tuxedos also we had time to breathe for a while. The next couple of days would be very busy, Didi's parents were coming in for the wedding in two week. We had to get a room ready for them, which means the boys would have to double up for a while. This was not a problem in anyway. Didi and Dawn wanted to pick up her parents so they went off together. The males stayed home talking about what to expect when we go through the rehearsals at the church. It was not long after the car pulled into the driveway, when Alex saw his grandparents he made a dash towards them giving them giving each a big hugs, and kisses.

The wedding rehearsals were coming up soon; Didi's father was giving her away we went in separate cars to the church. The priest put us through the ringer; every step had to be done right, on that day. We did it a couple times making sure everyone knew what was to be done. If they were not quite sure they asked questions, and the priest was glad to answer them.

The choir master was at hand also, and we had to pick the songs we want played, the readings was also picked, and Didi's mother said she would do a reading and Matt also agreed to do a reading. The rehearsal was over and at the end of the week it would be one week left before our big day.

The weeks flew by fast the big day came in like a storm, we got ready, and the males proceeded to the church. We were driven by my friend; the limo drove the Bride, bridesmaid, and her father to the church. The ceremony started on time, everything was perfect without any mishaps. When the priest announced husband and wife everyone clapped, and did the necessary signing of the book, walked down the aisle we were greeted with congratulations.

The reception was at the church hall we were very much surprise to see how well it was decorated the decorator did a wonderful job. The speeches were given, jokes told and whatever had to be said then a toast was given by Matt, and Didi's father which was amazing. I did not think Matt had it in him to make a speech as eloquent as the one he made today, which goes without saying you never know what one can do until they try.

We choose not to go on our honeymoon until a week later; Didi's parents decided they would stay with the children while we were away, and made arrangements to fly to Hawaii for a week. It was a beautiful day when we got there, but after a couple days it rained so we made ourselves comfortable inside, which we did not mind. We got to spend time with each other, it was the most spectacular show we had ever seen the last night of our stay, the hula dancers were tossing lighted torches and catching them with their bare hands without dropping any.

We returned to our rooms and, made love before leaving, holding each other in an embrace. We began feeling that gust of adrenaline, the passion, and ecstasy we had a beautiful experience having an orgasm together. It was a beautiful moment shared that night before returning home. We were picked up at the airport by a limo; we did not want her parents driving to get us. It was a surprise when the limo pulled into the drive way and we stepped out.

We got something for everyone, making them happy, in two days Didi's parents would be returning to Chicago, and they are welcome any time they choose to visit. The long summer holidays are here and Alex had to be registered for school. We made sure that was taken care off before anything else, so he and his brother could walk to school along with his friends, when he makes some after starting school.

At the start of the school semester Dawn is now in her twenties after graduating and is now attending university here in California, while the boys attend high school here Matt is in his late teens and would be turning seventeen when he graduates and would be attending university. He does not know which one but knowing him he would choose a good one, Alex on the other had has about three more years before graduating does not know at this moment which university he would attend.

It has been eleven years since we were married and everyone is doing great at university, Dawn is doing her internship at a hospital in the city, Matt is attending a university in Florida doing engineering and Alex is in Chicago attending the university there. He wanted to stay with his grandparents while he attend school studying bioethics, all is well with them, we hear from them twice a week letting us know how things are.

We are still married and doing great, the house empty, we find lots to do around the house there is gardening, grass to be mowed, and on occasions go hiking. The noise begins whenever the grown children comes for holidays, but have no idea when they would show up the house is always there and they each have a key, and can get in the house, without us being there. With that said the end is here, hope you have a good day.

Printed in the United States
By Bookmasters